CW01189595

SLAVIC MYTHS

SLAVIC MYTHS

Written by
Mila Fois

Illustrated by
Anna Schilirò

Translated by
Andrea Basso

SLAVIC MYTHS
«Meet Myths» book series
I edition: December 2023

All rights reserved. © No part of this publication can be translated, reproduced, copied or transmitted without the author's permission.

Written and published by Mila Fois

Illustration, arts, colors and design by Anna Schilirò

Translated by Andrea Basso

For all the news and a lot of mythology follow us on:

 Miti e Leggende

 meetmyths

Follow **Anna Schilirò** on:

 AnnettaArt

 annetta__art

PREFACE

It is difficult to find information about the multifaceted Slavic tradition, for two reasons. First, this tradition is rich in variants, since Slavic peoples have separated into different cultural groups, such as the Western Slavs (who became Poles or Czechs), southern Slavs (Bulgarians, Serbs, and Slovenes), and eastern Slavs (Russians, Ukrainians, and Belarusians). Second, this tradition has also often come in contact with neighbouring cultures, giving rise to many exchanges that have partly changed its fabric.

In the Slavs' culture and language, we can see Iranian influences and similarities with the Finno-Ugric populations, with whom they shared their territories. Moreover, we know of many contacts with the Byzantine Empire and its Orthodox faith. Finally, we should remember the intervention of the Viking-like Varyges who crossed the Baltic Sea in the 8th and 9th centuries and settled in the heart of present-day Russia and Ukraine. According to legend, the three brothers Hroerek, Sikniutr, and Thorvardr (whose Slavic names are Rjurik, Sineus, and Truvor) settled in Novgorod and later founded their own kingdom in Kyiv. All these cultures influenced the Slavic tradition, and we cannot ignore them.

Unfortunately, we do not have any direct sources of the Slavic pagan culture, and in order to understand this fascinating world of gods and spirits, we must rely on foreign authors such as the German Adam of Bremen, the Danish Saxo Grammaticus, Tietmar of Merseburg, and Otto of Bamberg. These sources always originate from ecclesiastical circles, often describing Slavic idols and deities from the strict point of view of evangelisers. However, these texts still give us helpful information about Slavic beliefs, which otherwise would have disappeared. We also find hints in the *Knytlinga Saga*, or *The Saga of the Descendants of King Canute*, by the Icelandic Olaf Tordson, son of the brother of the more famous Snorri Sturluson, the author of the *Prose Edda* and *Heimskringla*, another essential chronicle of Norwegian kings. A few Byzantine authors, such as Procopius, Constantine Porphyrogenitus, and Leo the Deacon, also provide valuable information in their registers, but they are always sparse and mostly of foreign origin.

The few Slavic sources we have are chronicles or sermons, the most remarkable of which is *Se pověsti vremjaninychŭ lětŭ*, also known as the *Primary Chronicle*. Here we find some useful information about the pre-Christian cult of the Slavs. Much has survived in popular folklore, but it is not easy to understand which stories have changed over time and which carry echoes of the originals. In 988, the Slavic peoples accepted Christianity, but this conversion led to the so-called *dvoeverie*, or dual belief, a mixture of pagan and Christian elements. On top of this, between 1700 and 1800, when nationalistic tendencies were developing, and many countries started looking for their myths of origin, the Slavs discovered that they did not have their own national chronicle; thus, they tried to remedy this lack by forging documents that were passed off as authentic pagan finds, when in fact they were just an attempt to provide their people with a national epic.

Many cultural and traditional elements have been preserved in the *byliny*, heroic songs dating back to the state of Kievan Rus', around the 10th century, transmitted orally and then transcribed and collected in anthologies from 1619 onwards.

As we walk through this labyrinth, where authentic sources are scarce, and much of the material comes from foreign or ecclesiastical chronicles, we will try to learn more about the fascinating and mysterious deities of the Slavic world, bearing in mind that our point of view will be that of mythology, telling the stories of gods and heroes who still today can awake our wonder and inspire us.

Thanks to all who will read these myths!

- MILA FOIS

Characters 1

Gods 9
Rod, Svarog, and the Creation of the World 10
Fertility Goddesses 12
The Children of Svarog 15
Veles and Perun, Fiercest Rivals 19
Dazhbog and Morana, a modern myth 23
Jarilo and Morana, Summer and Winter 28
Triglav and Svantovit, many faced gods 31
The White god and the Black god 34
Simargl, the Keeper of the Tree of Life 36
Chors, the Sun and the Moon 39

Heroes 41
Kurent, the Wine and the Moon 42
Kresnik among Horses and Goats, Wolves and Snakes 45
Volkh Vseslavevich, the Wolf Sorcerer 53
The Tale of Igor's Campaign 57
Dobrynya Nikitich and the Knights-Errant 62
Alyosha Popovich and Tugarin son of the Dragon 73
Mikula, the extraordinary Farmer 76
Ilya Muromets and the Last Giant 78
Why there are no more bogatyri in Russia 86

Mythological Creatures 91
Kapsirko and the Vodianoi 92
Marko Kraljevich and the Vile 95
The Hunter and the Rusalka 103
The Sword of the two Leshiye 106
Svarog and the Domovye 110
The Wolf and the Firebird 111

Finist the Falcon **115**
Marya Morevna and Koshei the Deathless **119**
Vampires and Werewolves **127**

CHARACTERS

Alyosha Popovich: one of the most skilled bogatyri, knights in the service of Vladimir of Kyiv. He was cunning, boastful, and loved women and good wine.

Baba Yaga: an old witch who often appears in folk tales. She flies around in a mortar and pushes herself around with a pestle. Sometimes she is helpful to the heroes or heroines, while at other times, she tries to hinder them.

Belbog: the white god, depicted in pale robes and with a long, white beard.

Chernobog: the black god, covered in metal armour, bringer of war, discord and disorder.

Chors: or Churs, a deity believed to be sometimes related to the sun, and others to the moon.

Dazhbog: solar god, believed to be the son of Svarog, who daily drives his chariot through the heavens.

Dobrynya Nikitich: valiant bogatyr in the service of Vladimir of Kyiv.

Dodola: or Perperuna, wife of Perun. Goddess who brings rain by milking her celestial cows, i.e. the clouds.

Dunai Ivanovich: knight in the service of Vladimir of Kyiv.

Finist: in Slavic folk tradition, he is a prince capable of turning into a falcon.

Igor: hero of one of the rare poems that give us helpful information about Slavic deities.

Ilya Muromets: devoted and brave bogatyr in the service of Vladimir of Kyiv.

Ivan Vyaslovich: a hero who must find the legendary Firebird, and succeeds in his quest thanks to the help of an extraordinary wolf.

Jarilo: god of the fair season and plant rebirth. Sometimes regarded as the son of Perun and Dodola raised by Veles, and others as the son Veles had from the abduction of Dodola.

Jarnik: or Vedomec, the antagonist of Kresnik, endowed with dark magical powers. In Slovenia, he is believed to be the Wolf Shepherd, the one who divides the herds and marks the end of the period when sheep can graze.

Koschei the Deathless: he appears in numerous folk tales as an antagonist. He is linked to Baba Yaga, and to kill him, it is necessary to find where his death is hidden.

Kostromo: male counterpart of the divine couple Kostromo - Kostroma, entities linked to fertility and spring.

Kresnik: Slovenian deity who later became a folk hero, connected to the horse and bringer of warmth and prosperity.

Kupalo: part of the divine pair Kupalo - Kupala, entities linked to the sun and fertile waters.

Kurent: Slovenian deity who later became a folk-tale hero connected to wine and drunkenness.

Lada: goddess of love and spring. She has a twin named Lado, and both are connected to fertility.

Lel: deity of love, son of Lada and brother of Polel.

Marya Morevna: warrior queen who managed to capture Koschei the Deathless. Ivan Tsarevich freed him by mistake and, together with Marya Morevna, set out to defeat him.

Mikula Selyaninovich: legendary peasant with great powers granted by Mother Earth herself.

Mokosh: mother goddess linked to the harvest, fate and spinning.

Morana: also Morena, Mara or Marzanna, goddess linked to death, as a moment of cold and sterility, destined, however, to end with the return of the good season.

Perun: thundering god, destroyer of snakes. He possesses a thundering axe that returns to his hands even if thrown far away; he shoots lightning-like arrows and travels in a chariot drawn by goats. The tree sacred to him is the oak, which attracts lightning more than any other, and his arch-enemy is Veles.

Polel: deity of marriage, brother of Lel, whose name means 'He who comes after Lel', because the foundation of a union must always be love.

Radigast: god related to strength, his temple was visited before going to war and divinations were performed there by means of a horse.

Rod: primaeval deity who created the world. The rozhanitsy of fate are linked to this god, connected to ancestors and destiny.

Stribog: deity of the air and winds, depicted as a tall and very slender entity with a thick beard and dishevelled hair.

Svantovit: god with four faces worshipped on the island of Rügen, linked to abundance, war and horses.

Svarog: ancient creator god, who put heaven and earth in their place and originated the other deities by striking the sacred Alatyr stone with his hammer.

Svarozhich: son of Svarog, the deity of fire.

Sviatogor: the last of the giants. He accompanied Ilya Muromets during his adventures, but his lineage was destined to disappear.

Triglav: god with three faces, his eyes covered by a blindfold, and his mouth gagged. Profound cosmic upheavals occur when these blindfolds are removed.

Vasilii Buslayevich: one of the last Bogatyri in Russia. Their arrogance led them to end their days turned to stone in the heart of a mountain.

Veles: god of the herds, also linked to the underworld, where he accumulates riches and leads the heavenly herds stolen from his arch-enemy, Perun. The two fight numerous battles, and Veles takes the form of a snake in this case, echoing one of the oldest and most widespread Indo-European myths.

Volkh Vseslavevich: a hero bearing the legacy of the ancient Slavic shamans, capable of turning into animals and performing wonders.

Zeleni Jurij: the Green George, solar dragon-slaying hero who was identified with St George.

Zhiva: goddess of life, linked to all earthly creatures.

Zlatorog: creature inhabiting the Slovenian mountains, described as a white chamois with golden horns. Its blood makes the Roses of Triglav blossom.

SVAROG	MOKOSH	ROD	SVAROZHICH
DAZHBOG	ZHIVA	MORANA	JARILO

SVANTOVIT   PERUN   DODOLA   VELES

RADIGAST   BELBOG   CHERNOBOG   STRIBOG   TRIGLAV

8

GODS

GODS

ROD, SVAROG, AND THE CREATION OF THE WORLD

According to the Chronica Slavorum by Helmod of Bosau, Slavic peoples had a primordial god known as Rod or Rodu. In earlier times, he was known as Deivos, a name that highlights his characteristics as a supreme deity. On the other hand, John Chrysostom associates the god Rod and his consort, Rozanica (who later evolved into a group of several entities, the Rozhanitsy), with destiny. When a child was born, offerings were made to Rod and the Rozhanitsy to help bring him into the world and ensure him a happy life. The Rozhanitsy were believed to appear in triads near the baby at midnight, three days after birth. The first of them, the youngest, spun the baby's destiny, the second had the task of measuring it, while the third, the oldest, would cut it, and the longer this thread was, the longer the baby's life would be.

Perhaps it is because of these connections with birth and destiny that Slavic folklore attributes the world's creation to Rod. He is sometimes depicted as the lord of the elements, standing on a fish, a symbol of the primordial waters, and adorned with a sash representing winds and air. In one hand, Rod carries a basket of flowers, born from the fertile earth, and in the other a wheel, symbol of the sun and the passing of time, and of the destiny spun by the Rozhanitsy. Legend has it that, in the beginning, there was only a large cosmic egg in which Rod was sleeping. Enclosed in the warm shell, the god dreamed, and in his mind, he already saw all that would be, admiring creation with his mind's eye. Finally, when the time came, Rod awoke, and as he stretched his numb limbs, he cracked the egg in two, thus originating light and darkness. The bright parts became the sky, the sun, and the stars, while the dark parts became the earth.

A majestic and mighty oak rose between the worlds; among its high branches was Prav, the divine realm; at the level of the trunk stood Yav, the earthly realm, while among its roots laid Nav, the underworld.

At the dawn of creation, Rod was alone, so the myth says that he desired a helper and gave birth to Svarog, the divine creator. Svarog raised the sky, separated it from the waters, and set the sun's path. At this point, however, there was no soil for earthly creatures to flourish, so Svarog threw the white, hot Alatyr stone into the primaeval waters. As soon as it touched the sea, the waters began to boil, becoming dense and compacted until they gave rise to the soil. But the ground was too heavy to stay afloat, and it sunk to the bottom of the primordial ocean. Thus, the earth had to be retrieved from the depths by two birds, or according to other stories by Rod in the shape of a sturgeon. A huge snake was placed underneath it to prevent it from sinking again. Mati Syra Zelmya, the Moist Mother Earth, thus began her ancestral and fruitful existence. However, another myth describes her birth in a way that is more similar to the Finno-Ugric version. In this case, the myth tells of a single islet that emerged from the primaeval waters, where a duck laid its egg. When the egg rolled down and landed in the water, it broke, and the upper part of the egg formed the sky and the lower part the earth. Given the similarities with elements of neighbouring traditions, it is likely that these Slavic legends are the result of some late interpolation.

FERTILITY GODDESSES

Mati Syra Zelmya, the Moist Mother Earth, is sometimes associated with the goddess Mokosh, the only goddess that, according to the *Primary Chronicle*, was worshipped on the hill of Kyiv, alongside the male gods Perun, Chors, Stribog, Dazhbog, and Simargl. Mokosh was a fertility goddess to whom women turned for help in childbirth or with the breeding of animals. She was especially connected with spinning, and when women heard noises coming from the spinning wheel during the night, they thought it was Mokosh helping them. With the advent of Christianity, Mokosh was not forgotten, but she became a domestic spirit who helped women with their tasks. In time she became identified with a Christian saint, like many other pagan deities that cannot be uprooted from popular tradition, and she became Svjataja Paraskeva Pjatnica, or St Paraskeva of Fridays. This saint was venerated on Fridays, and this detail may suggest that Mokosh, with her attributes of fertility and spinning, is connected to an archetypal deity like the Germanic Freyja and Frigg.

A spring stood among the roots of the cosmic oak tree, where Mokosh, accompanied by the Rozhanitsy, went to get water. The goddesses at her side were Dolja and Nedolja, or Sréca and Nesréca, Fortune and Misfortune. Due to their threefold nature, they are similar to the three Norns of the Norse tradition, who were also said to dwell at a spring between the world tree's roots.

Similar to the Germanic goddess Freyja and her brother Frey, a divine couple associated with fertility, are the Slavic gods Lada and Lado. Their names come from the Russian root lad, connected to harmony and union. They are part of a fourfold divinity linked to the harvest, widespread in folk songs and agricultural traditions, and each of the four aspects of this entity has, in turn, a male and a female part. Lado and Lada are gods of love, harmony and fertility, while Kupalo and Kupala were linked to beneficial waters, herbs and peace, and their

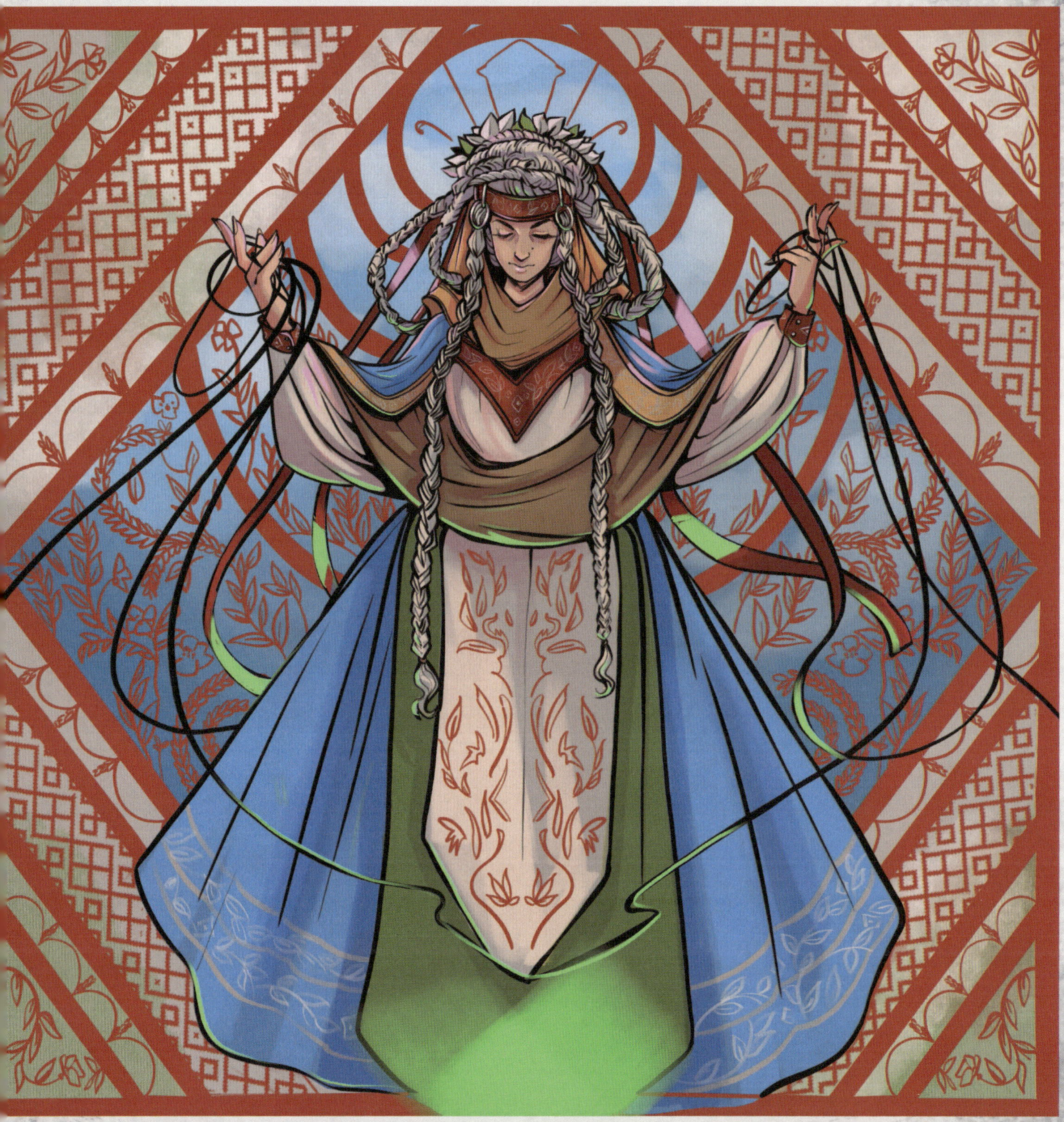

images were usually thrown into rivers to ensure prosperity. Then there were Kostromo and Kostroma, surrounded by horses and connected to wheat and agriculture, and finally Jarilo and Jarila, a divine couple related to the sun, or sometimes the moon, and the rebirth of plants in the good season.

According to a recent tradition, it was Lada, together with Svarog, who gave birth to the human race, laughing and playing in the woods, throwing pebbles which came to life once they touched the moist and fertile soil. The stones thrown by Svarog became the first men, and those thrown by Lada were the first women. According to a 17th-century text, the goddess also has two sons, who are twins as well: Lel, a young man similar in some respects to the Roman Cupid, with blond curls and capable of arousing feelings of love in people's hearts, and Polel, the goddess of marriage, whose name means "Coming after Lel", indicating that love should always come before marriage. The archaeologist Boris Rybakov believed that Lada also had a third daughter, Lelya, a beautiful maiden connected with spring.

In Belarusian tradition, there is a story of a beautiful rose covered in timid dew, kissed one day by a ray of sunlight. Thus, Lada was born, the beautiful maiden of joy and springtime, who immediately turned into a swallow and flew over the entire country, bringing harmony and prosperity. Sometimes, Lada and Lelya appear alongside Mokosh as her daughter and granddaughter.

Another goddess linked both to the fertility of the soil and to the cycle of life and death is Zhiva, mentioned by Saxo Grammaticus and Helmod. This latter describes the cult of Zhiva, whose name seems to mean "The Living One", as rooted in the heart of a forest, near a sacred spring. She was also called Zevana or Devana, and she was similar to Diana or Artemis. She often carried a bow, and her sacred animal was the bear, highlighting her connection to hunting, to the wild creatures that lived in the deep forest, and to the delicate balance between life and death that hunters must never forget. Zhiva was also associated with the saint Paraskeva, and her holy day was Friday, linking her to the archetypal fertility goddess common to other cultures. In Slovenian folklore, she is also known as Vesna, a spring goddess.

When we talk about birth, we should not forget the other side of the coin: life always comes with death, just as summer is followed by winter. The goddess who recalled this concept was known under many similar names: Marzanna by the Polish, Marena by the Russians, Morana by the Bulgarians and the Serbs, Mara by the Ukrainians and Belarusians, and Morena by the Lithuanians. In agrarian rituals, she was burnt or drowned at the end of winter, as she represented the forces of frost, sterility, and death, and she had to be driven away so that Kostroma, Lada, and the other goddesses of the fair season could be reborn to bring prosperity and fertility. Zhiva and Morana are sometimes considered two aspects of the same goddess, representing nature that dies and then blossoms again.

THE CHILDREN OF SVAROG

On the Alatyr stone, located on the primordial island of Buyan, the god Svarog engraved the first laws, which would regulate the lives of all creatures. Svarog was thus a law-giver god, and the *Primary Chronicle* presents a bizarre fusion with Egyptian antiquity, drawing on a type of narrative like that of the priest Manetho. According to this story, after the Flood and the fall of the Tower of Babel, a certain Feostu reigned over the earth; the Slavs knew him as Svarog, and in the text he is equated with the Greek Hephaestus. He was thus a god of forging, a blacksmith connected to the element of fire and creation. When his pincers fell from the sky, human beings, still living in a primitive state, learned to forge metals and create weapons and tools. But Svarog is also a celestial god, and he forged the sky, as the Finnish Ilmarinen is said to have done. According to folklore, Svarog struck the white stone Alatyr with his hammer, and the sparks it produced gave rise to numerous gods.

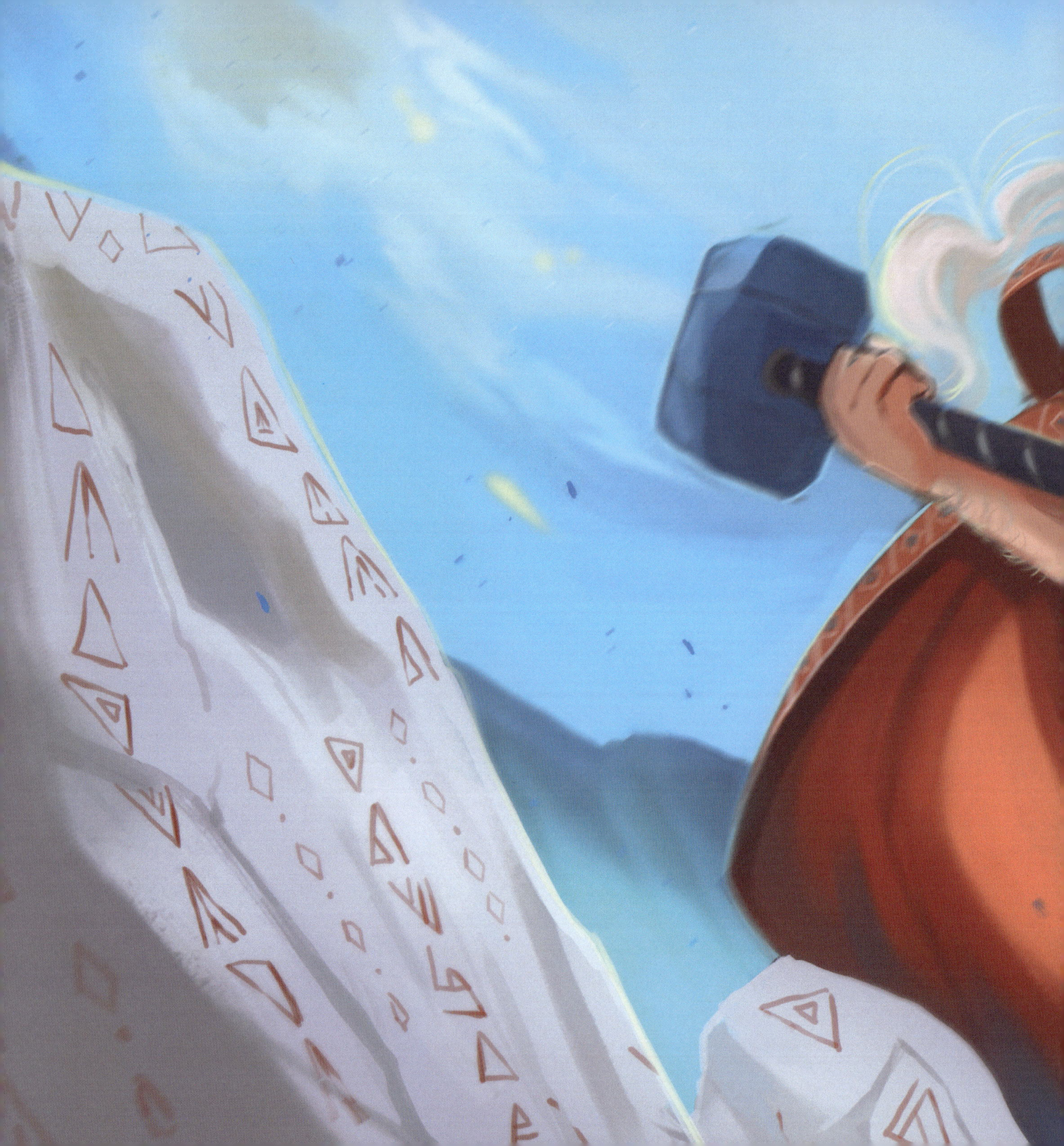

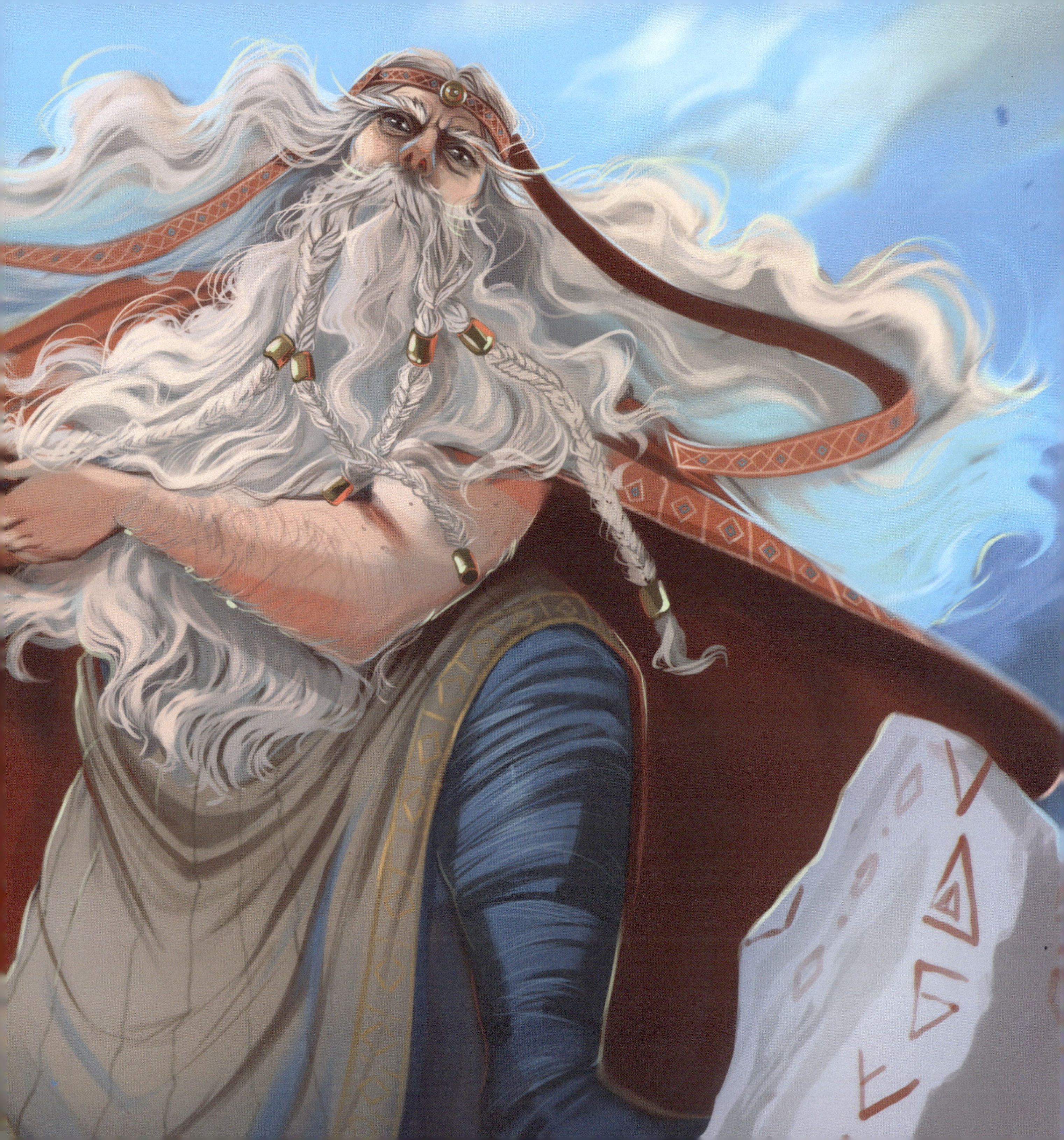

The Svarog of the *Primary Chronicle* also brought laws to humankind, who still led uncivilised lives, mating without ties and not even recognising their children. After the god's intervention, monogamy was established, and the people of the world began to live in a dignified manner. In this case, the god is the one who forges unions and marriages. In the end, Svarog handed over power to his son, whom the Slavs called Dazhbog, the Bestower, and who is assimilated in this text to the Greek Helios. There are similarities between the two deities: Dazhbog, like Helios, is said to travel through the sky in a solar chariot driven by four white horses, and to dwell in the east, crossing the heavenly vault every day along the path set by his father, until he reaches the west. His glittering shield gave off a glow that could blind those who stared at it, but the closer he got to the end of his journey, the more the shield got covered in dust, becoming opaque and pale. This is how a popular legend explains why sunlight weakens as sunset approaches. Because of this connection with the solar cycle, a popular saying was that in winter Dazhbog died, but first, he locked the earth with keys which he gave to the birds, only to retrieve them in spring when they returned, ready to be reborn and light up the world with his warm light. Every day at dawn, his daughter Zvezda Dennitsa (also known as Zorya Untrennyaya), the Morning Star, would help him prepare the horses and tie them to the cart, while every evening, Zvezda Vechernyaya, the Evening Star, would take care of the horses and bring them to rest. A popular legend relates that, on the day of the summer solstice, Dazhbog would ask his daughter to tie three horses to the cart, instead of four, so that they would travel more slowly across the heavens and shine for longer than usual, which is why the summer solstice is the longest day of the whole year.

Svarog has another son, Svarozhich, related to the element of fire. It is said that, when the solar Dazhbog goes to rest after his long journey through the sky, Svarozhich's time comes, ready to brighten and warm the evenings of humanity with his benevolent flame. He dwells in a granary, where a dim torch burns to make the grain dry, and for a long time the offerings to the god consisted of grain. Once, when the night was still dark, and humanity lived in a primitive way, Svarog took pity on those creatures trembling with fear and cold and hurled a thunderbolt at the earth. He struck an oak tree, which flared up at one, flames blooming on its branches like crimson flowers. The humans picked up one of the branches and carried the fire to their homes. Knowing that Svarog had created it, they called it Svarozhich, the Son of Svarog or Little Svarog. The Slavic peoples had the utmost respect for fire: no swearing was allowed in its presence, and anyone who threw dirt into the flames was despised.

VELES AND PERUN, FIERCEST RIVALS

Veles, or Volos, is an extraordinary god, endowed with many and sometimes divergent aspects. He is described in the sources as the protector of cattle, as a chthonic god, as the lord of wealth, prophecy and poetry. He is sometimes depicted as a dragon or a serpent, especially when fighting his arch-rival, the thundering Perun. Sometimes he has the head of a bear instead, or he has the shape of a snake with a bear's snout. He is also depicted as a hairy horned god. He is connected to the crop, and according to some accounts, during the harvesting of wheat, people would take a handful of ears of grain, tie them together and thus form an object of sacred significance. This bundle was believed to be "Veles's Beard", and it was considered blasphemous to touch it; its purpose was to protect the harvest. Veles has a cunning personality; he is a charmer and a deceiver, and he is connected to magic, which has always been linked to music and poetry. According to Vittore Pisani, these aspects make him similar to the figure of the Greek Hermes, a god as quick as the wind, sharp-thinking and smooth-talking, who also plays the role of the god of thieves and psychopomp, he who accompanies the souls to the underworld. He has also been likened to the Norse Odin, himself a patron of poetic inspiration but also capable of cunningly deceiving his enemies, and lord of the departed warriors who gather in Valhalla.

The Lithuanian counterpart of Veles is called Velnias, and he can help us to understand this deity better. Not only is Velnias in constant conflict with the thundering Perkunas, but he is also described as having only one eye, just like the Norse Allfather Odin. One of Velnias' epithets is Ragius, the Seer, and in many Lithuanian folk tales, drinking from the spring containing "Velnias' waters" confers the gift of clairvoyance.

The names of the volchvi, the Slavic sorcerers and shamans, is said to derive from Veles, and with the decline of paganism his traits were inherited by a hero of folk ballads known as Volkh Vseslavevich. Unfortunately, we know very little about Veles, and parts of his mythological cycle have been reconstructed by Russian philologists Vyacheslav Ivanov and Vladimir Toporov, using traditional Slavic and Lithuanian songs and tales, as well as through comparative study.

While the temples of Veles, a chthonic god, were built in the valleys, those of his rival Perun, linked to the sky and the storm, were erected on the hilltops. We have many attestations of a thundering god known as Perun, endowed with silver hair and a thick golden beard, crossing the sky on a chariot drawn by one or more goats and summoning lightning with his darts or by hurling his axe, which always comes back to his hands. In this description, he is similar to the Scandinavian Thor, whose archenemy is the serpent Jörmungandr. The *Primary Chronicle* tells us that the Russians made their oaths by invoking Perun and Veles, so the myths concerning these two characters must have been well known, although only a few attestations have reached us. Because of his ability to dominate the elements and to fly through the sky on a chariot, in Christian times Perun was identified with Saint Elijah. We can find one of the many examples of Elijah commanding the weather in the First Book of Kings, where the prophet states: "There shall be neither dew nor rain, except when I say so". We know that, in

988, Vladimir converted to Christianity and ordered the statues of pagan idols to be thrown into the river Dnepr. Many mourned, seeing the figure of Perun carried away by the currents, eventually sinking into what is still known as the Perun Deep.

Veles and Perun were always enemies: Veles stole the herds from the surface and led them to his chthonic realm, prevented the rain from falling or, on one occasion, kidnapped Perun's wife, but the thunder god always managed to recover the stolen goods, defeating his adversary with thunderbolts. A folk tale tells of a time when the people of the world stopped sacrificing to Veles, and the fire in his temple turned to cold ashes. Outraged and determined to punish humankind, Veles prevented all springs from bringing water to the surface, leaving men and beasts at the mercy of droughts and epidemics. A crow, flying over the villages and seeing the miserable conditions in which the people lived, decided to warn Perun and ask him to intervene. The thundering god climbed into his chariot, inciting the goats to run as fast as they could to the underground abode of Veles, the great serpent. He shot his deadly, blazing arrows, and the thunderbolts fell from the sky, making the whole earth rumble and passing very close to the coils of his enemy. Veles took refuge in a hollow tree, but Perun's thunderbolts soon made it burst into flames; the serpent then sought shelter behind a rock, but the darts of his enemy split it into pieces. Then Veles realised he could not win and agreed to return to his chthonic realm and free the waters from their captivity, making the fields fertile again. At that point, from the highest branches of the oak tree that formed the cosmic tree, Perun shouted: "That's it! That's your place, stay down there!" proclaiming his own victory.

According to legends and folk songs, Perun had a wife named Dodola or Perperuna, a goddess of rain who milked her celestial cows, the clouds, and made water fall on the lands of men. One day, Dodola went for a walk in a clearing, and there she met Veles, who abducted her and took her with him to the underworld. According to some interpretations, it was on this very occasion that, together with Dodola, Veles conceived Jarilo, a god related to the hot summer who

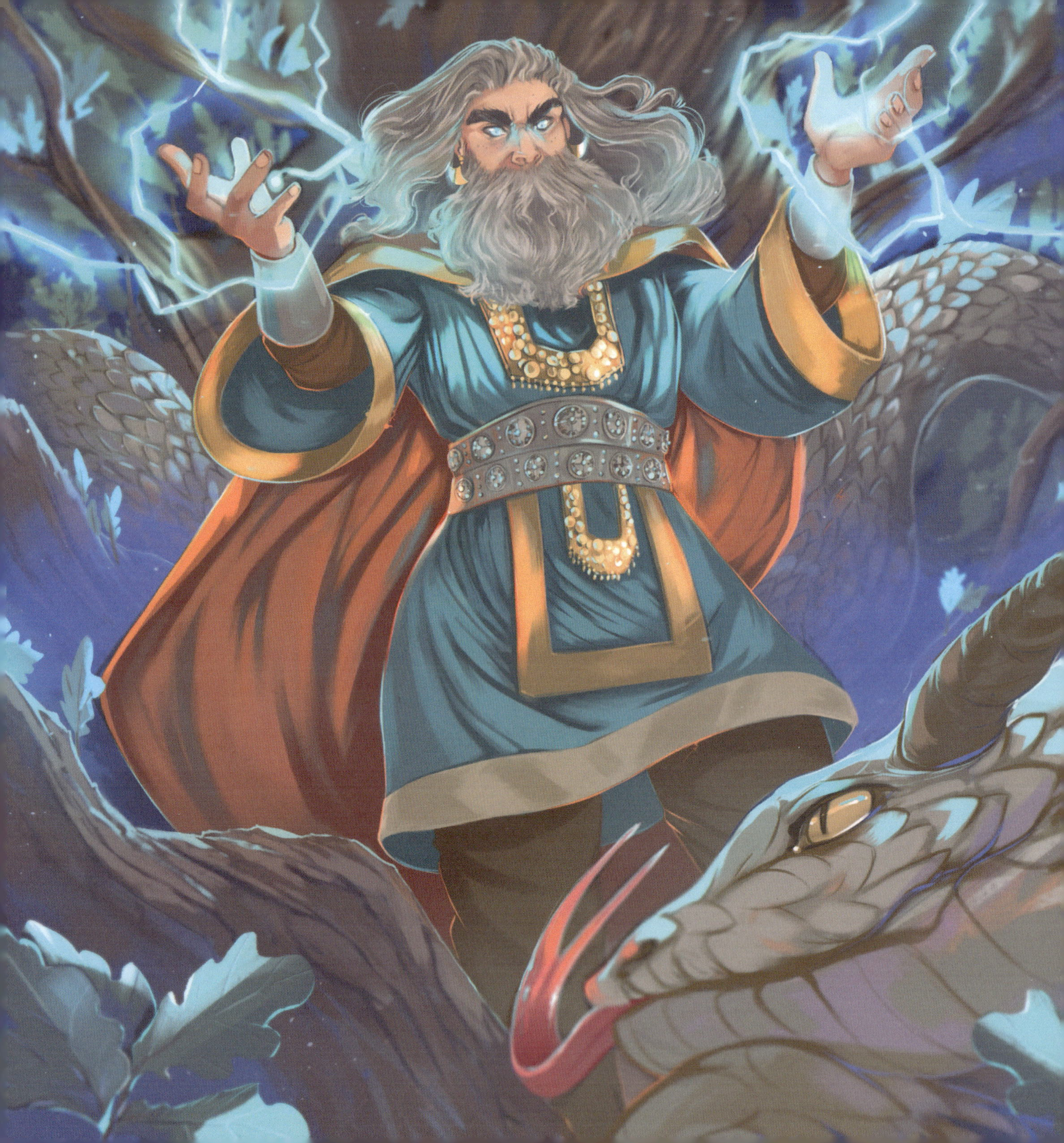

is considered Perun's son, but who was raised by Veles in his chthonic realm, and perhaps the reason for this is concealed in this legend. Naturally, Perun did not willingly accept the abduction of his beloved, and armed with thunder and lightning, he waged war on his rival, in a terrible battle that lasted for three days and nights. Finally, as usual, the stormy god prevailed, and Dodola returned with him to the realm of the gods, while Veles remained confined in the underworld. Then, returning contentedly among the highest branches of the cosmic tree, like an eagle finally subduing the serpent, Perun exclaimed again: "That's it! That's your place, stay down there!" as a Belarusian fairy tale goes.

DAZHBOG AND MORANA, A MODERN MYTH

Veles' misdeeds were not over, however, as the herd god believed he could take better care of the celestial cows than anyone else, so he captured them one by one and kept them underground. Perun did not confront him alone this time, but he enlisted the help of the solar god Dazhbog. The two descended among the roots of the great oak, and there they found Veles lurking in the form of a huge snake and not intending to come out. Perun, easily angered, drew his own blazing axe and started shooting his darts of light towards the roots of the cosmic tree, but Dazhbog had to stop him, for in doing so, he risked destroying the sacred oak that supported the whole world. "Challenge him to a duel! If you are one-on-one, you will see that he will accept and come out of his hiding place. In the meantime, I will seek the heavenly cows!" suggested Dazhbog, letting the two rivals fight it out between themselves. The outcome was the same as always: Perun's thunderbolts sent Veles fleeing, and the horned god, well aware of his limitations and not too offended, meandered away. Shortly afterwards, the thunder god heard Dazhbog's voice coming from beneath his feet. The solar god had found the herds, but they were confined underground. Another of Perun's powerful thunderbolts was needed to crack the earth's crust. The god then swung his axe, and with a radiant blow, charged with electricity, he opened a crack in the ground, thus allowing the clouds to return to their rightful place in the heavens.

This story continues in a more modern version, where the deities present characters and elements typical of the Slavic *byliny*, traditional narratives with heroes, princesses, and ferocious beasts. In particular, this account incorporates aspects of the story of Marya Morevna. We can see that these modern reconstructions use deities in place of folklore characters, while keeping the narrative core of the ballads intact. Throughout history, the opposite is often the case: divine entities are gradually stripped of their powers and transformed into folk heroes or benevolent spirits, or even assimilated into Christianity in the form of saints. Using the gods as protagonists of these stories is an attempt to restore a national epic and a cohesive Slavic mythology. However, we must remember that these are 18th-century reconstructions, which draw on mythical material in order to find a unity that has now been lost.

In this modern variant, the story tells of how Dazhbog, while roaming the chthonic realm in search of the stolen cows, reached a seemingly abandoned palace where he found a man in chains. Thinking that he was another victim of Veles's ticks, Dazhbog freed the mysterious man, who revealed himself to be Koschei the Deathless, one of the most recurring antagonists within the *bylina*. Too late did Dazhbog realise what he had done, and by then the damage was accomplished. Koschei, however, was grateful to the god who had freed him, and promised to help him three times.

When the sun god returned to the surface, the weight of that mistake still haunted him, and perhaps it was because of this that the dark Morana managed to approach him. She was the one who had captured Koschei and confined him down there, and since Dazhbog had thwarted her plans, he felt indebted to that goddess of winter and death, and he agreed to spend time with her. Zhiva, the huntress goddess, tried to warn him that no good could come of Morana, yet Dazhbog did not listen to her; he was seduced by the dark cold goddess and began to lose his solar power. Morana, on the other hand, bore no love for the shining Dazhbog, and when he rested at night, exhausted by the constant travels on his solar chariot, the goddess would go to the chthonic realm to meet her lover Koschei and plot some new mischief with him. The couple also had two daughters: Karna, the dark goddess of grief and weeping, and Zhelya, the messenger of death, who flew over the battlefields to collect the ashes of the dead, which she kept inside a horn.

When Dazhbog found out about Morana's nightly escapades, still ensnared by her enchantment, he descended to the underworld to fight his rival. Still, he was weakened by the plots of the goddess of death and was therefore wounded and defeated. Koschei could have easily killed him, but he remembered that he had promised to spare him three times. Nevertheless, Dazhbog did not give up, and after bathing his wounds in the fountain of Life and Death to heal completely, he was ready to resume the fight. Two more times did Koschei prove to be the strongest, but spared Dazhbog again to keep his promise. But when the solar god had exhausted all his chances, Morana intervened and decided to keep him as a prisoner in the lower realm. The sun, hidden in the darkness of the nether realm, stopped shining its light upon the living beings, but luckily Zhiva had already sensed the dangers that the sun god was facing. She turned into a swan and flew to the roots of the cosmic tree to save him, despite the icy, baleful draughts that Morana had sent against her. She managed to free Dazhbog and bring him back to the surface on her white, feathery wings, while Morana was punished and burnt by the fire from Svarog's forge, which consumed her until she became a hideous old hag.

Filled with hatred and resentment, Morana decided to enact the final phase of her evil plan, revealing to Dazhbog the only way to kill Koschei the Deathless. Between the roots of the great oak tree lay a secret chest, and in that chest was a hare, inside which was a duck, which in turn contained an egg. In the egg's fragile but well-protected shell lay Koschei's soul. All Dazhbog had to do was to break it, and his rival would die at once. The solar god immediately set out in search of the chest, against the warnings of the cunning Veles. According to him, Morana had made that revelation for a dark purpose, so it would be wiser to leave the egg alone. In his wounded pride, however, Dazhbog sought blind vengeance, paying no heed to the warnings of other deities, and he broke the shell of the egg. A thundering crack then filled the air, and with it, Koschei perished. But that was not all, for the cracking of the egg also made the golden blindfold that covered the three heads of the god Triglav, hiding his eyes and holding his mouth shut, fall to the ground. The primordial deity Rod himself had blindfolded Triglav at the very creation of the universe, because he knew that the entire cosmos would be plunged into chaos if Triglav were to look at the three realms with his three pairs of eyes and simultaneously speak with his three mouths. Triglav was the guardian of the three worlds, but now that the golden veil had fallen, the god shouted angrily with three different voices, breaking down the barriers that kept the three realms separated from each other. The subterranean waters rose and swallowed up the whole land; only those who sought shelter in the mountains were safe. Morana had succeeded: the world was in total despair.

But Rod had not created it all only to see it end like that. He turned into a golden sturgeon and went to look for the earth, which had sunk beneath the primeval sea, and he managed to bring it back to the surface. Then he placed the blindfold over Triglav's eyes and mouth once again, and he asked him to guard the three worlds and never again allow them to overlap. The gods worked to restore the balance and make the land prosperous again, and Dazhbog finally managed to forget the cold, wintry Morana. He was once again shining with all his might, and he became the progenitor of a new humanity.

This tale has no direct counterparts in the oldest sources. It imaginatively mixes the deities of the Slavic world and the heroes and villains of the *byliny*, heroic narratives that hardly ever feature gods as protagonists but rather focus on the young sons of the tsar or on the *bogatyri*, the knights-errant of medieval stories. Nonetheless, some fragments of ancient mythology still manage to surface. We find the sun, represented by Dazhbog, captured by the goddess of winter and sterility, only to return strong and bright at the end of the season. We find the theme of Koschei's death, typical of many Slavic narratives, and a few known characteristics of other deities such as Triglav, which we do not find in actual narratives, because these tales were rather a product of the nationalisms that arose in the 18th century.

JARILO AND MORANA, SUMMER AND WINTER

The slavist Radoslav Katičić has recently attempted to reconstruct the myth of Jarilo, and the following is his story.

Jarilo was the *desetnik*, or tenth son, of the thunder god Perun. According to Slavic folklore, *desetnik* or *desetnica* are special children whose status as the tenth child put them more in touch with the forces of the unknown, leading them to fulfil an extraordinary destiny. Jarilo was also born at a particular time, namely during *Velja Noć*, the Great Night, when the Slavic peoples celebrated the New Year. On the very night he was born, the child was abducted by dark, chthonic forces and taken to the underworld, the realm of Veles. This god was the arch-rival of Perun, Jarilo's father, and perhaps he had commanded the child's abduction. According to other interpretations, Jarilo was instead the son of Veles and Perun's wife, conceived when the goddess had been abducted and taken to the underworld, and for this reason Veles had ordered him to be taken to his realm as soon as he was born. In any case, Veles raised him in his underworld domain, where he watched over many herds as a cattle god. Jarilo was put in charge of looking after Veles' animals, which according to many stories had been stolen from the surface. Every spring, however, Jarilo was allowed to return to the surface, and it was then that the flowers bloomed and spring came.

The first person to notice his return to the sun-kissed realm was Morana, herself the daughter of the god Perun. Jarilo and Morana thus formed a pair of divine siblings, and it is not surprising that they fell in love and married, bringing great fertility to the world. Even Veles and Perun, at this point, moved by the affection and union of the two young people, stipulated a truce, and then the whole earth could enjoy a long period of peace. Jarilo, however, was a fertile god of agriculture, and perhaps one woman was not enough for his exuberant fecundity. This is why he proved unfaithful, and when Morana found out, she was so angry that she killed him. As we have seen, this goddess represents the forces of winter,

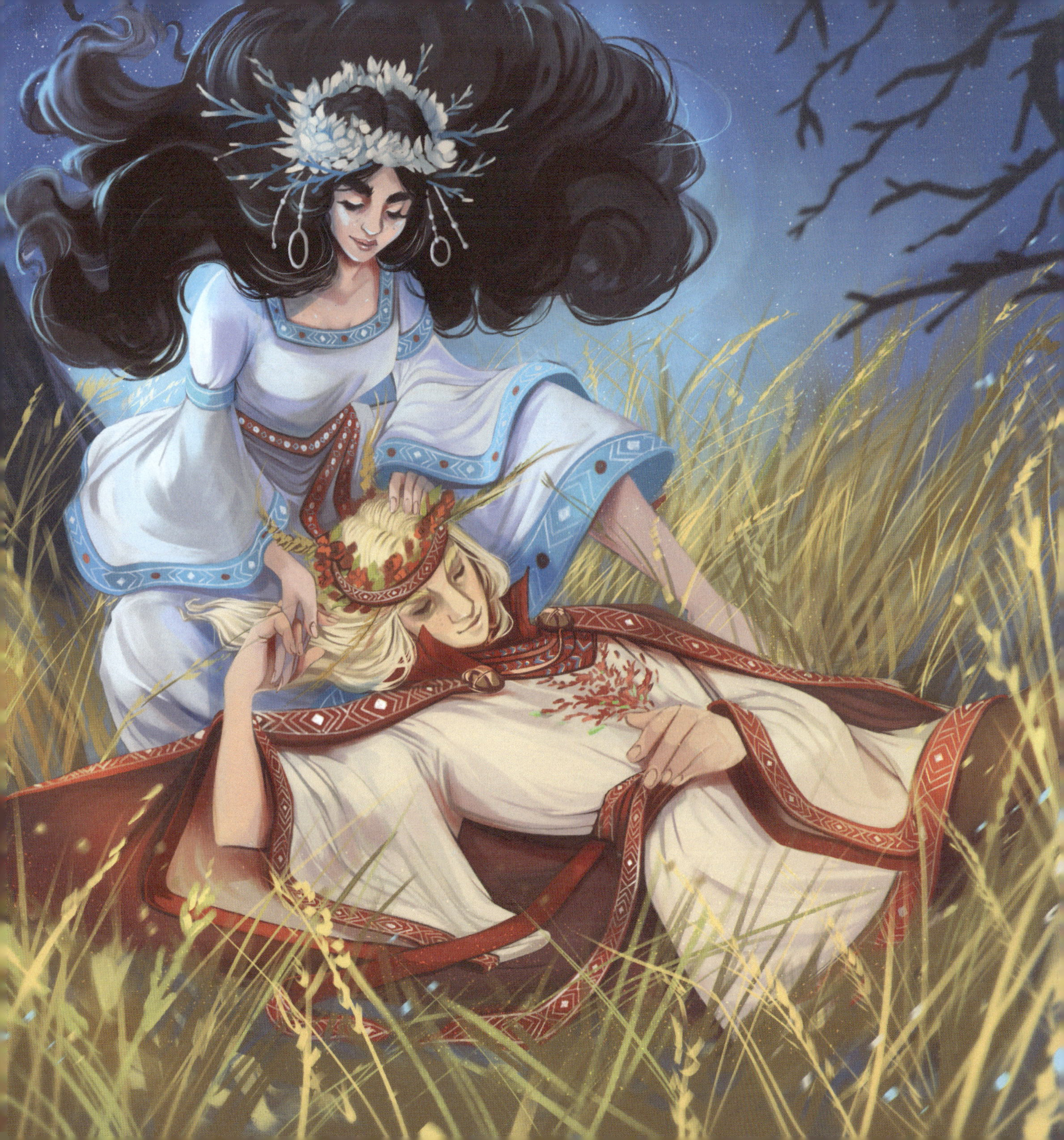

and it is not surprising that she is the one to kill the solar Jarilo. Morana's blood crime deeply affected her, turning her into a cold, bitter, hag-like goddess, the perfect embodiment of winter. Even in her new form, grief consumed her, and in fact she did not live long, perishing at the end of the cold season. When the new spring came, both Morana and Jarilo would be reborn, and the cycle would begin again, their actions bringing about the changing of the seasons.

Jarilo was also associated with Zeleni Jurij, the Green Saint George, a hero linked to the sun and vegetation, protector of livestock and slayer of a cruel and dangerous dragon. The fight between the serpent and the sun god is a mytheme that seems to belong to all cultures (we can think of Apollo and Python, Indra and Vritra, or Ra and Apophis). In this case, St. George gives a Christianised and thus more acceptable appearance to the fight between Perun and Veles, after the conversion of the Slavic peoples.

Morana is closely connected to Zhiva, the goddess of spring, sometimes also called Vesna, who represents her solar aspect, before the grief over Jarilo's death transformed her. These two goddesses are often seen as two sides of the same coin, two interconnected but profoundly different seasonal aspects.

TRIGLAV AND SVANTOVIT, MANY FACED GODS

The tree at the centre of the world was an oak, and between its branches were the three different worlds: the celestial, the terrestrial and, between the roots, the chthonic. There was a three-headed god linked to these three worlds, and his name was Triglav, He Who Has Three Heads, which according to the Archbishop Ebbon of Rheims represented the three realms. According to one of Otto of Bamberg's biographers, Triglav was depicted with a golden sash covering his eyes and mouth, as he did not want to see the evil deeds done by men or to have to report them to the other gods. In the city of Volyn, when Otto tried to eradicate the pagan faith, the people hid the golden idol of Triglav and entrusted it to a widow who lived in the countryside, hoping it would not be discovered. The woman concealed it inside a hollow tree, allowing only the faithful to go there to pray and make votive offerings. Otto, however, heard about this, so he sent a trusted man, who knew the local language, to ask to pray to the idol, with the secret intention of removing it. According to the chronicle, the statue of Triglav was so well embedded in the hollow of the plant that it could not be moved, and so the man had to go back without having succeeded in dismantling the cult of the three-headed god.

Triglav also has a female form, known as Trigla, which in turn has a triple aspect. She is often identified with Mokosh and is also known as Zlata Baba (Golden Grandmother) or Pethra Baba among the Slovenians. The latter appellation links her to the bright Alpine goddess Perchta, who leads the night procession of spirits just as Zlata Baba leads the *Divja Jaga*, the Wild Hunt.

For the South-Eastern Slavs, Triglav corresponded instead to the god Trojan, who wore a black cloak and rode a black steed in the night. In some folk legends, he avoided the rays of the sun, and if caught outside shortly before dawn, he would hide in haystacks to avoid being burnt by the sun.

At least four temples were dedicated to Triglav. They are described as marvellous works of art, adorned with sculptures of men, birds, deer, and other animals, so skilfully crafted that they looked alive, and coloured with such mastery that not even the weather could ever ruin them. In addition, precious objects from the spoils of war would be presented as votive offerings on his altar.

Some scholars liken the figure of Triglav to Svantovit, a four-headed god worshipped by the Polabian peoples. Each head looked in a different direction and had a different colour: the one looking north was white, the one looking west was red, the one looking south was black, and the one looking east was green. Svantovit was a god connected to prophecy since he could see everything, but also to divination and war. Saxo Grammaticus describes the idol located in the temple of Arkona, with four faces with beards and shaved hair, with a bow in one hand and a metal horn that was filled with wine every year in the other. How much wine remained until the following year determined the fortune and well-being of the community. A saddle and bridle were kept in this temple, as well as a colossal sword with a silver scabbard and hilt. It was such a sacred place that only the priest, who, unlike all the others, had a long beard and long hair, could enter it, and even he had the duty to hold his breath so as not to contaminate the sanctuary. Svantovit also owned a white horse, located in an enclosure near the temple, and it was believed that he rode it during the night to fight against his enemies. Because of this, in the morning, the horse's coat was often dirty with mud and foam, as if it had travelled great distances and made great efforts. This animal was also used to perform divinations: before going into battle, spears were planted on the ground, and the horse was made to pass through them. It was considered a good omen if it started with its right hoof, or if it managed to pass without moving any of the spears.

The cult of Triglav also included the presence of a horse near the statue of the god, but in this case it was a black-coated animal. Svantovit was one of the most beloved gods of the Polabian peoples, and it was difficult to overcome their veneration of him and lead them towards Christianity. Perhaps this is why Svantovit was likened to Saint Vitus, as was often the case throughout the history of conversion, whereby a saint took upon himself the attributes of a god, thus gaining the people's loyalty. According to hagiography, Saint Vitus had to escape pagan persecution, and he saved himself by fleeing by sea, fed by an eagle that swooped down to offer him food. Svantovit was a god of war but also of abundance, he had similarities to the Perun of the Eastern Slavs; eagles were sacred to him and were depicted on a banner in his temple. If we consider how eagles played an important role in St. Vitus' life, we can understand why, as Christianity grew stronger, the saint took the place of the god.

There was another deity whose cult involved divination by means of a horse that had to pass through spears, and his name was Radigast, who perhaps took this appellation from the name of the place where he was worshipped. He was depicted with a swan on his head, a symbol of wisdom and sharp thinking, and with the muzzle of a bull engraved on the shield he carried against his chest, a sign of strength and steadfastness. His temple had several gates, one of which led to the sea, so close and violent that it was terrible to behold. It was supported by the horns of different animals, at least according to a description by Tietmarus, and guarded the golden statue of the god, protected by a fearsome armour. The Slavic peoples would visit this temple before going to war. They believed that, to herald the coming of troubled times, an enormous boar would emerge from the waves of the sea near the temple, roaring among the currents.

Saxo Grammaticus recounts the sack of Arkona by the Danes, two of which were charged with the task of destroying the idol of Svantovit. This foreign god instilled such reverential fear that they were afraid of arousing his wrath, so they ordered the slaves to break down the statue, so that the wrath of the god would fall onto them. When the colossal statue collapsed to the ground, a demon in the form of a black animal was seen fleeing from it. At that point, the Danes were able to take possession of the rich treasure accumulated in the temple, the fruit of years of devout veneration.

THE WHITE GOD AND THE BLACK GOD

Helmod's chronicle reports a custom of the Slavic peoples, which consisted of passing a cup full of liquor to each other and, amidst exclamations and incitements, stating that all good came from the good god, and all evil from the black god, whom they called Chernobog. Because of this, it was assumed that there was a god who opposed the black god and was the bearer of good: a white god, Belbog. Although this is only a supposition, Monica Kropej noted that many Slavic and Balkan peoples had a deity known as Belibog or Belinez, perhaps a transposition of the continental Celtic god Belenus. Peisker's theory, on the other hand, identifies the rivalry between these two deities as a theme in Persian mythology, where the bright and good god Ahura Mazda is in perpetual conflict with the cruel and dark serpent Angra Mainyu. According to Ivanov and Toporov, on the other hand, the two gods would enact the battle, widespread throughout all Indo-European cultures, between a god with solar qualities and an evil dragon that tried to deprive the world of its well-being and prosperity. Although no studies can definitively confirm these theories, the two rival deities became part of the Slavic pantheon, at least on a popular level. Belbog was portrayed as a typical good god, with a long white beard and snow-white robes, wielding a staff with which he was said to summon rain by striking the clouds. On the other hand, his antagonist, the black Chernobog, was covered in a dark, metallic armour, and he brought chaos and destruction wherever he went.

What follows is a narrative that does not come from an ancient mythological corpus, since, as we have seen, we have none concerning the Slavs; rather, the story stems from modern popular folklore, which from the 1700s onwards was used to construct a unified Slavic epic. In this story we find that Chernobog, in the form of a dark serpent, decided to extend his dominion over the world of light, but he met with immediate opposition from Svarog. The god took up his blacksmith's hammer and repeatedly struck Alatyr, the white stone that had been placed on the earth at the time of creation. The sparks emanated by the stone gave life to the deities that would help Svarog in his struggle against the serpent. Hence Stribog, the god of the winds, was born, along with the solar Dazhbog and Simargl, who appears as a winged dog. But Chernobog was no less powerful, and in turn, he crashed his serpentine tail against the Alatyr stone, emitting sparks that became demons and creatures of darkness. A terrible battle loomed between gods and scaly monsters, but Svarog locked himself in his forge, asking the other deities to hold back the black god's forces, to give him time to create a weapon that could end the battle. Everyone expected Svarog to appear with a sword, a spear or a similar object, but instead, the god emerged from the forge with a golden plough. The great serpent was subdued, crushed by the plough and trapped underneath it, and so were all his children. Chernobog then surrendered and promised Svarog that he would remain quiet in his territories, making the god of forge realise that a boundary had to be drawn. Using the golden plough, Svarog traversed the entire middle realm, establishing that the territory of the gods would remain under his rule, while the chthonic territory belonged to the serpent's line. However, as far as the earth's surface, the object of the battle, was concerned, Chernobog was to remain on the left side, while the right side would be destined for Svarog's sons.

In this narrative we can find references to the Finno-Ugric epic, where Ilmarinen, a blacksmith and a creator that forged the heavenly vault, finds himself on a series of challenging quests to marry his beloved maiden. One of these requires him to plough a field teeming with poisonous and deadly snakes, and the blacksmith solves the matter by making a plough with a golden vomer, with which he crushes and subdues the reptiles. The ancient struggle between the serpent, bearer of darkness and disorder, and the god who finally makes cosmic order triumph remains the same across many different mythologies.

This story has also been transposed into the Christian tradition. Indeed, we find a Ukrainian legend concerning the saints Kuzma and Demyan, or Cosmas and Damian, also known as the physician saints and connected to the forge (from the term *kuznya*, resembling Kuzma's name). The two saints are said to have created the first plough, so large that it could only be pulled by a dragon. The giant reptile was chasing the tsar's son, but the boy managed to reach the forge of the saints, where the plough had just been completed, and he asked for shelter. Cosmas and Damian offered protection to the young man and harnessed the dragon to the plough, which made the deep furrows known to this day as *Zmievy Valy*, Walls of the Dragon, a line of defence located below Kiev. The two saints were believed to be able to forge not only extraordinary artefacts, but also marriages so strong that they would never break, which is why women would look for husbands on the day they are commemorated, *Matushka Kuzma-Demyan*.

SIMARGL, THE KEEPER OF THE TREE OF LIFE

In the *Primary Chronicle*, Simargl is described as one of the deities worshipped on Kyiv Hill, along with Perun, Dazhbog, Stribog, Chors, and Mokosh. In the same source, Simargl is said to have the form of a bird, or a winged dog, and to be the keeper of the world tree. Scholars have made many assumptions about the nature of this deity, who, in one sermon, even appears as two different entities, Simu and Riglu. These could be two aspects of the same deity, or form a divine pair, or it could just be a mistake made by the copyist. Since we have no further written evidence, it is not easy to give a definitive answer. Simargl's appearance might, however, come to our aid, as in the Persian tradition there was a sacred bird called Simurgh that appeared with the feathers of a peacock, the claws of a lion and the muzzle of a dog. It was a wise and benevolent creature whose nest was on top of the cosmic tree in the centre of the universe. This tree stored the seeds and fruits of all good things that could grow on the

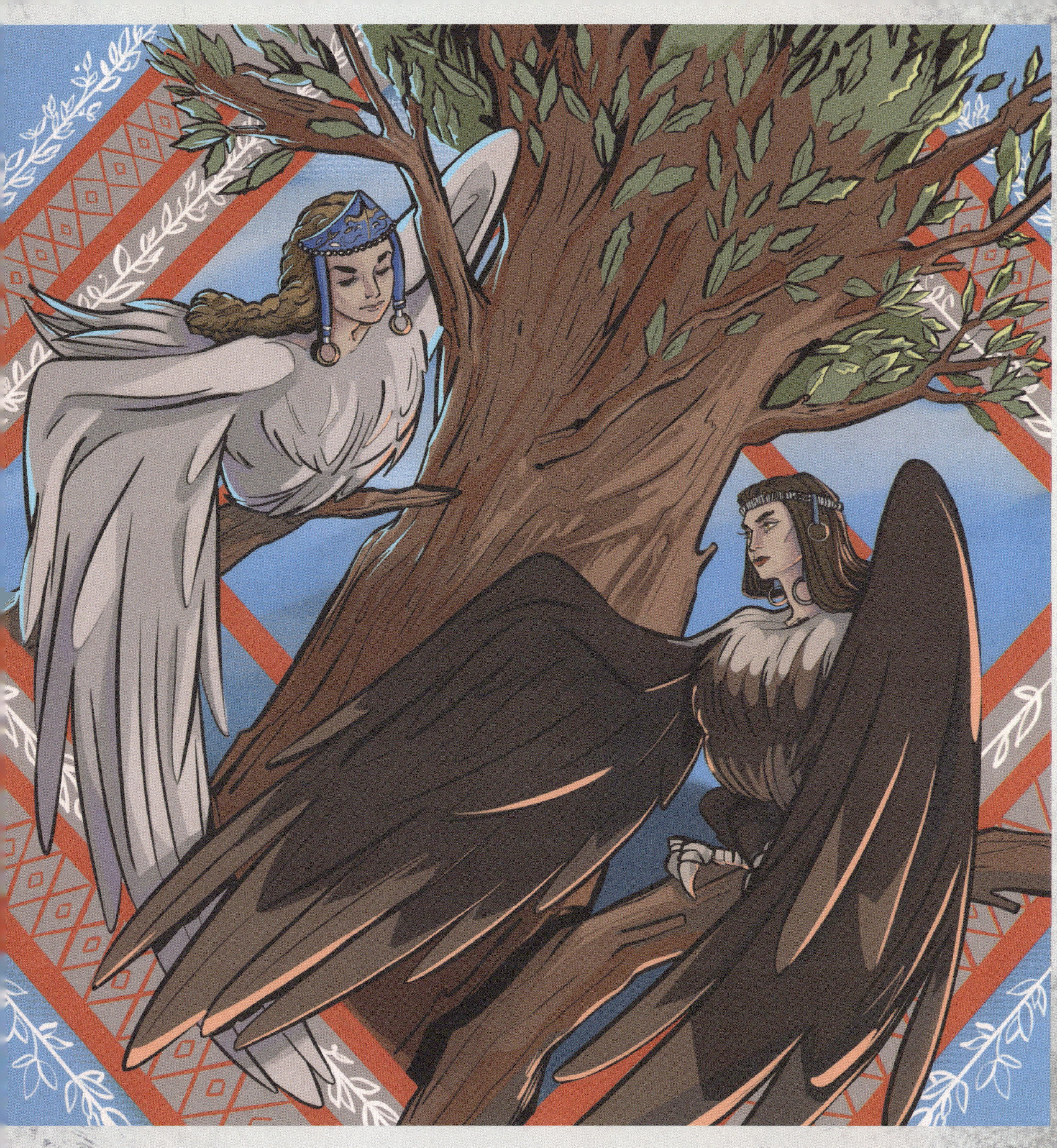

earth, and when the divine bird took flight, these spread everywhere, making the soil fertile. Knowing these details about the Simurgh, Simargl's description in the *Primary Chronicle* seems to make sense. In the Slavic world, the tree of life was often depicted with two guardian creatures, similar to gryphons, and this could be the reason for the confusion and splitting of Simargl into Simu and Riglu. These two birds could also be the representation of Alkonost and Sirin, two mythical creatures with a bird's body but a woman's torso and head, similar to the Greek sirens, who were said to sing in the lower realm, bewitching the listeners with their melancholic voices and making them forget everything.

CHORS, THE SUN AND THE MOON

Chors, or Churs, is one of the six deities who had an idol on a hill in Kyiv, and we know even less about him than about the other Slavic deities. Based on our sources, he seems to be a solar god, which is why he is sometimes identified with Dazhbog, although the two seem to have different characteristics. While Dazhbog is anthropomorphic and crosses the sky on his chariot, Chors was the personification of the Sun as a star. Some see in this a vague resemblance to the Egyptian Horus, but others associate Chors with the Moon instead. The reason for this interpretation is found in certain verses in *The Tale of Igor's Campaign*. Here, a sorcerer prince is described running in the shape of a wolf before the cock crows, along the road of the great Chors. The Moon is usually linked to the transformations of werewolves, creatures widespread in Slavic folklore and known as *vulkodlak*. Moreover, running in the middle of the night, the sorcerer prince could only run along the course of the Moon. Without enough elements to settle the dispute, we cannot know for sure whether Chors was therefore a solar or lunar god, although we do know of a solar Iranian deity known as Khorshid that might provide some clues.

In a modern-day narrative, Chors is described as a white horse that would bring light into the world, galloping every day to the high heavens. In this respect, he resembles the Norse Skinfaxi, the white steed driving the chariot of Dagr, the personification of day. It is said, however, that during the night, when Chors did not illuminate the earth, human beings felt lonely and afraid. Thus, the solar god answered their prayers and struck the clouds with his own mighty hooves, giving rise to many sparks of light, which became the stars. From that moment on, the shape of Chors' hoof also remained impressed in the heavens as the Moon. Although this tale does not come from the oldest sources, it does point to the fact that the white horse was identified with the sun in many cultures, especially Slavic ones. This is clearly demonstrated by the folk heroes Kresnik and Zeleni Jurij, alongside the solar Jarilo himself, who carried on the oldest of battles, the fight for light and the beautiful season, waged between Perun and Veles or their counterparts throughout the world.

HEROES

HEROES

Slavic folklore is full of interesting characters who often appear to be heroes developed from an older original core, in which they were considered deities instead. Since we have so few sources on the Slavic pantheon, the considerable heritage of traditional stories, ballads and songs comes to our aid.

KURENT, THE WINE AND THE MOON

Kurent is a much-loved hero in the Slovenian tradition. He is still remembered on the day dedicated to St. Martin, the saint who inherited this folklore figure's characteristics. On this day, the time when the flocks are left to graze ends. On Shrove Tuesday there is a large carnival parade in which the kurenti, *the famous horned masks, covered in fluffy sheep's wool, appear, wearing large cowbells around their necks to chase away the cold and winter. There are many folk tales, anecdotes and songs about them, and Janez Trdina has collected them during his travels in Serbia and Croatia.*

Once upon a time, when the world was still unformed, a rooster laid a huge egg, which cracked open and gave birth to everything. Seven great rivers flowed from its cracks, and humanity lived in a kind of earthly paradise, in a beautiful valley surrounded by mountains. The rooster had not gone away, but he crowed every day, marking the hours of the day and warning men and women when it was time to wake up, eat or go to sleep. At first, they were grateful to him because they were still primitive and would not have known how to organise themselves, but as time went by, they began to get tired and to consider that rooster and his constant crowing a significant nuisance. Finally, they unanimously decided to send him away, and the rooster agreed to leave, but not before giving his final warning: "Watch out for the lake!" The men did not understand this suggestion and gradually began to lose their good habits, sleeping late, forgetting to forage for food, and living lazily and inconclusively.

Their inactivity led them to chatter on silly subjects and to have strange ideas, such as that of going all together to the great egg, which still made the seven rivers gush forth, and breaking its shell, in order to obtain more water. So they took stones and began to throw them at the cosmic egg, which soon broke, releasing a huge wave that swept over everyone and reached the valley, thus creating a lake. The rooster had warned them, but the men failed to understand his message. Only one man survived, fleeing to the high mountains, but even there he was in danger, because the water level was constantly rising. He considered climbing on a tall oak, but the flood had covered even those majestic trees. The only foothold he found was a thin vine twig, and he clutched it with all his strength, hoping it would not break and praying that he could save himself. Kurent, who was wandering the world with a vine-stick, noticed the man clinging to it and, with his powers of regeneration, caused the stick to lengthen, rising above the level of the flood and carrying the unfortunate man to safety, all the way above the clouds. When the waters finally subsided and the land was dry again, the man thanked Kurent for saving him, but the god shrugged, with an enigmatic smile, "It is not my doing, but the vine's, so you should rather pay tribute to it!" Since that day, indeed, the vine has been one of mankind's most beloved plants, and its product, wine, is held in high esteem and is a favourite among all drinks.

Kurent is an extravagant character, appearing in folk tales as a cheerful, witty fellow who can even cheat death. He has a magic flute, and when he plays it, no one can stop themselves from dancing frantically. He is a god connected to ecstasy and wine, which is prepared precisely in the autumn period when the king of the *kurenti* is traditionally elected. These horned and hooded figures chase away the cold during the period called St. Martin's Summer, when winter seems to diminish for a while, after which it will continue to freeze the world until Shrove Tuesday. Kurent originally enjoyed divine status, and many scholars associate him with the Greek Dionysus, who in turn is linked to wine and drunken frenzy, and both figures are also connected to the bull. In a tale from the Christian era, God and St. Peter, in order to punish the sinful Kurent, turned him into a bull and offered him to a farmer without demanding anything in return, saying only that, after seven years, they would come back for him. Kurent, in bull form, worked hard, ploughing the fields and making them so fertile that they began to produce an enormous amount of fruit, vegetables, and grain. The harvest was so rich that no one went hungry anymore, but there was no need to buy provisions either, because everyone lived in total abundance. Full of joy, the villagers led the bull in procession around the village, celebrating together, and it was then that God and St. Peter returned to take him back. "Remember these happy times, especially when this very day comes!" they said, returning Kurent to his true form and letting him go. This happened on the day known as Shrove Tuesday, and the abundance brought by Kurent in the form of a bull has been remembered ever since, with processions, dances and festivities. When Christianity began to spread, Kurent became an increasingly irreverent character, so much so that, in some stories, he is admitted neither into Heaven nor Hell, and finally decides to go to the moon, where he is identified with the man who, in many cultures, is said to live up there and can be detected in the moon spots.

KRESNIK AMONG HORSES AND GOATS, WOLVES AND SNAKES

The figure of Kresnik is very dear to the Slovenians. He was once a sun god, linked to the summer solstice, called kresni dan *in Slovenia, but he later became a dragon-slaying hero. In this latter incarnation, however, we can still recognise the ancient myth of the shining god fighting a snake, like Perun against Veles. The tales that follow have been collected by Pohorski, Trstenjak, and Kelemina.*

Like many other heroes destined to perform extraordinary feats, Kresnik was not born quickly, but his mother carried him for nine long years. When the child finally came into the world, it was clear that there was something strange about him, as he had a horseshoe-shaped mark on his skin. In other versions of this story, he had horse hooves instead of feet. Kresnik was also a *desetnik*, the tenth son (which in some accounts becomes the twelfth or thirteenth), so he had a special connection with the forces of the afterlife. His family owned several cows, and the boy used to take them out to pasture, marvelling at the excellence of their milk and fearing that someone might try to take them away. On a warm, sunny day, Kresnik milked one of the cows and got his fill; satisfied, he lay down under a tree and fell asleep. When he awoke, he noticed that the meadows around him were empty. He looked behind the thick bushes and climbed on some high rocks to get a wider view of the valley, but he could see no trace of his animals. The herds had been stolen! Kresnik searched for them restlessly, unleashing his faithful four-eyed dog, which could see better than anyone else. Finally, the hound began to bark, scratching the ground at the foot of the mountain, as if he wanted to dig a tunnel and descend underground. Kresnik realised that his animals had been brought down there, so he turned into a bird and flew over the rocky peak, looking for a passage to the core of the earth. He discovered that an enormous dragon had trapped his cows under there. Filled with rage, he hurled a bolt of lightning at the reptile, killing it and thus being able to bring the precious herds back to the surface. In this folk tale, ancient elements of the myth survive. It resembles the moment in which Perun descends into the chthonic realm to retrieve the celestial cows, carried away by

Veles in snake form.

Other stories link Kresnik to the reptilian world. The Serpent Queen, a wicked enchantress who had learned the dark arts in Babylon, had arranged a feast in honour of her daughter, and Kresnik and his brother Trot were going to join in. The two climbed aboard their golden chariot, capable of soaring through the air. It was drawn by white steeds, while the hooves and the quick wheels made the entire vault of heaven roar like a thunderstorm. The Serpent Queen thus became aware of their arrival and sent one of her servants in the shape of a serpent with eagle-like wings to get rid of the two troublemakers. Among the clouds, Kresnik and Trot could not see him coming until it was almost too late, as the gaping jaws of the reptile emerged from the white curtain. At the last second, Kresnik managed to duck and avoid being devoured, and Trot had the quick wit to grab his axe and slam it down hard on the snake's long neck, chopping his head off. As the headless body writhed horribly, its tail hit the clouds, which thickened and became dark and storm-laden. Lightning struck the two brothers' chariot, and the incessant rain nearly drowned them. The two had to keep low, sheltered at the bottom of the chariot, to avoid being hit by the lightning, but at the same time, the water was filling it and did not allow them to crouch for too long. Luckily, the horses were swift and managed with enormous effort to pull the chariot, which was getting heavier and heavier, out of the storm and away from the dark clouds.

When they were close to the Snake Queen's palace, the brothers realised that the guards would never let them in, especially not after they had killed their pursuer. However, Kresnik wanted access to the vast halls at all costs, not least because he had heard that the daughter of the Serpent Queen was beautiful, and that the queen herself possessed the most precious diamond crown in the entire world. So he took one of the horses off the yoke and rode it bareback with extraordinary skill, so quickly that nobody saw him reaching the castle. Once there, he turned into a dwarf, so as not to be recognised. The guards let him in, but everyone made fun of him at the feast because of his hideous appearance and short stature. Paying no heed to their insults, Kresnik could not look away from the beautiful princess and her mother's glittering crown. During the games and celebrations, he decided to take action, challenging the snakes to run faster than a wheel he would roll down a hill. The queen also wanted to join in, but the dazzling crown would have slowed her down, so she took it off and left it at the top of the hill, ready to spring forward as soon as the bizarre dwarf pushed the wheel down the slope. So the game began, and all the snakes set off in pursuit, determined to win the race, while Kresnik took the opportunity to seize the crown and take the princess with him. Soon, however, the theft and kidnapping were noticed, and the Snake Queen sent her entire army of venomous reptiles after the thief. Kresnik ran down a narrow corridor, hearing the snakes slithering along the walls and seeing them getting closer and closer. Keeping a cool head, he closed all the metal doors along his way, to hinder his pursuers, and finally came to safety.

Sometime later, as he rode swiftly and proudly across the moors, feeling at one with his steed, he could not fail to notice the tall towers around which a gigantic serpent had coiled. He was biting its own tail and forming an impenetrable barrier around the walls, surely guarding something precious. Kresnik asked the locals about the mysterious reptile, and he learnt that it had been standing guard for six months now, keeping Princess Vesina prisoner. It was St. George's Day, and Kresnik decided to rescue the maiden. Galloping on his white steed, sword in hand, the hero charged at the monster and managed to defeat it. He chained it to a rock, where, according to legend, it remains trapped to this day. Thanks to his heroic act, Kresnik freed the beautiful Vesina and married her, but the story does not end with a happily ever after. Although Vesina, who bore the attributes of Vesna, the goddess of spring and the awakening of nature, was delicate and gentle, the charm of the snake princess had not ceased to enchant Kresnik. According to some tales, the hero would ride at night, as fast as the wind, to visit the seductive princess. When Vesina found out, catching sight of him from behind as he set off on his escapade, she called him by name. This was enough to kill him on the spot.

In these tales we find many echoes of the ancient mythology. The fact that the solar hero is unfaithful to his wife and is killed for this reason is also part of the story of Jarilo. The wheel that Kresnik rolls down the hill to deceive the snakes resembles a typical summer solstice custom, the letting loose of flaming wheels down the hillsides to ensure the prosperity of the land. Given his solstitial character, it is not surprising that Kresnik was likened to St. John with the coming of Christianity, but his exploits as a dragon slayer also make him similar to St. George.

Regarding Kresnik's death, there is a different legend that includes an anti-hero called Jarnik, the Green Hunter, Trot, or Vedomec. He was a hunter but also a sorcerer, the dark antithesis of his brother Kresnik, embodying the power of night as opposed to the forces of daylight. In Slavic folklore, this figure sometimes led the *Divja Jaga*, the Wild Hunt, during the twelve coldest and darkest nights of the year, also known as Wolf Nights, when the clatter of ghostly hooves could be heard in the sky. Kresnik and Vedomec would turn into animals and fight a sort of shamanic battle. Still, in the end, the solar hero will be treacherously killed by his dark brother, just as summer finally succumbs under the bites of the cold winter. In this case, the figure of the solar hero merges with that of Zlatorog, a legendary unicorn-like being, represented either as a white horse, a chamois, or a goat, endowed with golden horns. The hooved figure of Kresnik was inextricably linked to the horse, and his overlap with Zlatorog is not surprising, as a personification of the thundering Perun, a god who drove a chariot drawn by goats. In any case, this mythical animal with solar attributes is known especially in the Slovenian regions, where there is a mountain with three peaks known as Triglav, after the ancient three-headed deity. On this mountain dwelt the White Ladies, endowed with a profound knowledge of herbs and capable of making pastures green, as well as provoking avalanches and severe thunderstorms when angered. Protected by these good ladies, Zlatorog lived on the highest peaks, in the form of a white chamois with golden horns, or a stag, or even a unicorn. His horns were said to be the only key to open the mountain and find the treasure that was guarded by a terrible multi-headed serpent. For this reason, many hunters, especially the Green Hunter, the personification of winter and dark forces, tried to kill him. Luckily, this was not an easy task, for from the blood spilt by Zlatorog, miraculous red flowers called Triglav's Roses would blossom and immediately heal any wound. Zlatorog would eat them and soon return to strength, so that no one could take possession of his golden antlers. One day, a gold seeker climbed the mountain searching for precious materials and ended up in a cave guarded by a terrible reptile that hissed with its three heads, preventing anyone from approaching the treasure stacked behind it. The man hid, trying to figure out a way to bypass that dangerous creature, when he heard the clacking of mighty hooves. Zlatorog had entered the cave and, after approaching the snake, had touched it with his golden horns. Immediately the reptile became tame, and the gold seeker understood the secret to obtain those riches. However, he dared not harm Zlatorog, perceiving it to be a sacred creature, so he followed it from afar, until he saw it scratching its horns against a tree. Near the scratched bark, he found a small fragment of horn, enough to appease the snake and take away some small treasure. Once home, however, he found that his fiancée was not satisfied, "You were lucky enough to see Zlatorog and you didn't even bring me one of the famous Triglav's Roses! You don't really love me!" The man, eager to please the maiden, took up his gun and returned to the top of the mountain, in search of the white, golden-horned chamois. While walking along a path, he met a mysterious hunter in green clothing who offered to help him. "I know where Zlatorog has gone, follow me and we will find him!" he exclaimed, leading the seeker through rough paths known only to himself, until, in the distance, Zlatorog's splendid silhouette stood out. "Take aim and shoot at the heart!" suggested the Green Hunter. The man, however, only wanted to spill a few drops of blood, just to seize the Rose of Triglav for his beloved; he did not want to kill the sacred creature of the mountain. He shot and wounded the creature, which immediately leapt away, but the hunters were at its heels, marvelling at the trail of beautiful red flowers that had blossomed wherever Zlatorog blood fell. The treasure hunter stopped to pick them up, declaring himself satisfied, but the Green Hunter urged him to keep going: "We must shoot again, before that creature can eat one of the flowers and regenerate! Come on, don't tell me you're not interested in its golden horns, capable of opening the mountain gates and revealing all kinds of riches!" Greed got the better of them, and the two resumed their chase after Zlatorog, but they found him healthier than ever. Indeed, while they were speaking, the creature had eaten one of the roses and had cured itself completely. As soon as he realised the hunters were approaching, he bravely faced them, charging them head-on. The gold seeker tried to dodge, but the sun shone and reflected off the animal's horns, dazzling him. Backing away without looking where he stepped, he ended up in a precipice, still clutching the small bunch of red flowers to his chest. At that point, the Green Hunter burst into an evil laugh, as Zlatorog leapt away, and this time for good. They say that nobody has ever met him again, and that the White Ladies, outraged by the attempt to harm their favourite creature, have turned the mountaintop from a fertile land full of pastures and healing herbs into a barren and dangerous place. They also say that the fiancée, in distress because the boy had not returned home for days, went to the riverbank, where she saw his now lifeless body still clutching the bouquet of red flowers he had picked for her.

The fight between Kresnik and his dark double, known as Jarnik or Vedomec, is reminiscent of the fight between Zlatorog and the Green Hunter, who is chasing him to kill him. This motif has become so widespread in popular folklore that people believe that children born with some particular sign, such as still wrapped in placenta or bearing some mark, or even the tenth children of the same couple, are *kresniki*, shamanic figures endowed with a connection to the world beyond, able to travel in dreams or to separate their souls from their bodies to perform some mission of fundamental importance for the well-being of the community. The *kresniki* also periodically face a battle that pits the forces of light and warmth against those of darkness and cold, fighting against the *vedomci*, the dark sorcerers derived from the figure of Vedomec. They can be recognised because they are born with some special sign, and when they are seven years old, they are led at night, like sleepwalkers, to a crossroads or un-

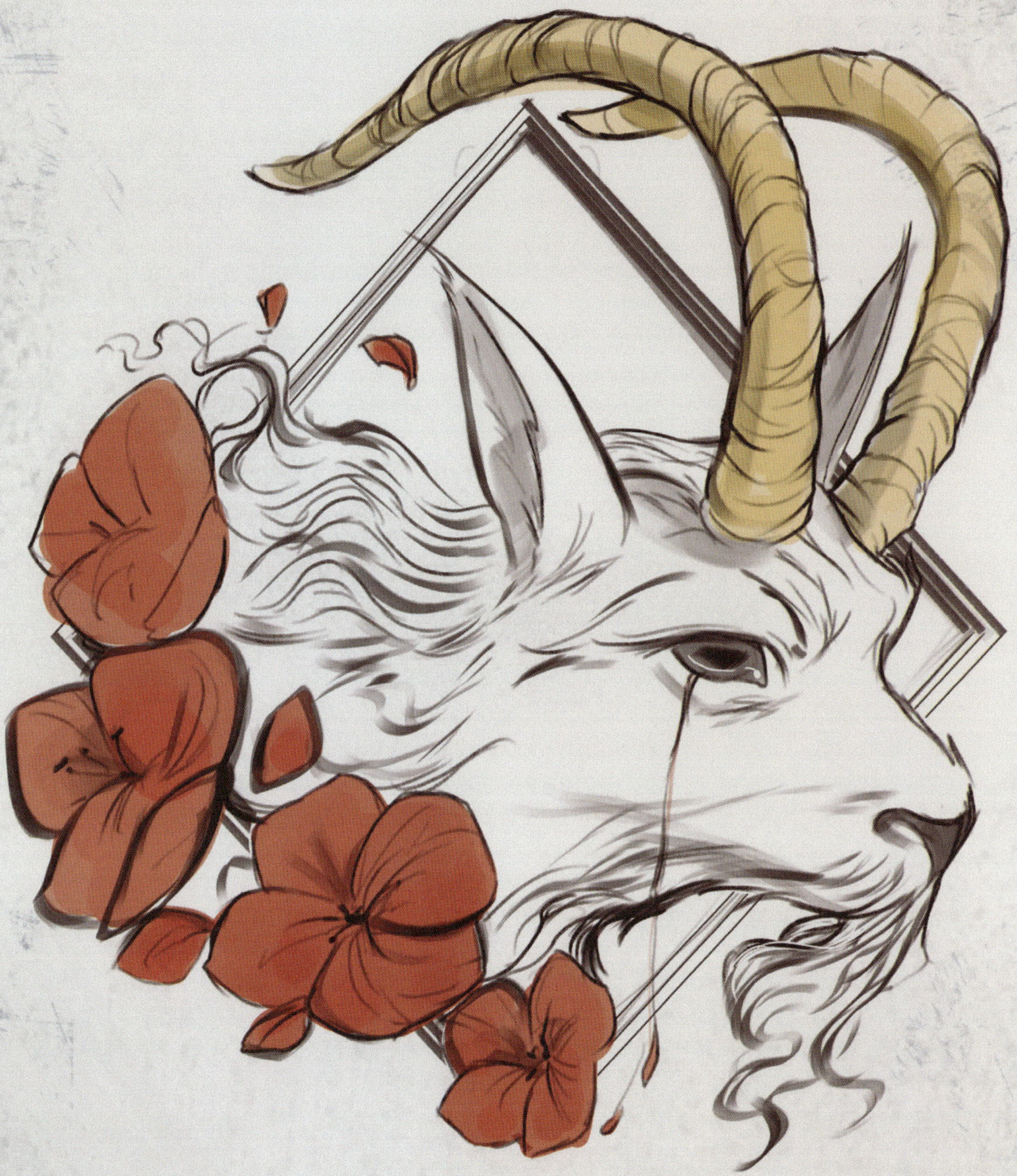

der a large oak tree, where they are welcomed by the other *vedomci*. From then on, they come out of their bodies at night to perform their evil deeds, such as souring milk, cursing people or beasts, or uprooting plants. But the moment of the great battle against their bitter rivals, the *kresniki*, occurs on Midsummer Night, where the flashes of lightning seen in the distance, even when the sky is clear, are believed to be the signs of this ancient magical struggle. They often fight in animal form, and peasants can help the *kresniki* when they see, for example, a white dog, wolf, ox, bear, or boar fighting with an animal of the same type, but with black fur. They must, however, be careful to strike only once, as the second blow would only make the *vedomci* regain all their strength. To keep these negative entities away, Slovenian peoples used to hang garlic in front of doors, scatter salt or holy water, a type of protection traditionally used against vampires or werewolves, sometimes connected to the *vedomci*.

Another figure similar to Kresnik and Jarilo is Zeleni Jurij, the Green George, who on St. George's Day rides a white steed and rescues a maiden held captive in a castle guarded by a dragon. His rival, called Jarnik, Jurij s pušo (George with a gun) or Volčko, is regarded by Slovenians as a Wolf Herdsman. At a certain time of year, when the cold weather arrives, all the wolves are said to gather in one place to await this figure, who arrives on the back of a goat or, in other legends, in the form of a white wolf, and would then divide them into various packs, sorting the different hunting territories among them. Zeleni Jurij would start the season when the herds can graze, on St. George's Day (23 April), while the Wolf Herdsman would mark its end, on St. Martin's Day (11 November). The Wolf Herdsman appears as an eternal wanderer, riding a goat or a wolf, and is often lame or blind in one eye. He appears especially in winter, and despite being the lord of wolves, he is considered a protector of herds. In the Christian world, he is associated with Saint Blaise, the same saint and shepherd who is also identified with the ancient god Veles, himself a guardian of livestock. Once again, the struggle between Perun and Veles returns, this time represented by Zeleni Jurij, the slayer of the dragon, and Jarnik, the Wolf Herdsman.

VOLKH VSESLAVEVICH, THE WOLF SORCERER

Volkh Vseslavevich (or Volga Buslavlevich) appears in the Slavic byliny, *tales based on real events, but reinterpreted in a fantastic way. Bylina could be roughly translated as "What once was", as if to say, "Once upon a time". The figure of Volkh could be inspired by that of the historical prince Vseslav of Polotsk, considered to be a sorcerer and a werewolf, while his name means shaman, priest, or sorcerer, an enchanter belonging to Slavic paganism.*

It was night, and one of the largest moons ever seen was shining, when Volkh Vseslavevich came into this world. The stars turned red, as if spilling blood, and a mighty earthquake shook the earth. The animals were terrified and fled to their dens, howling and screeching madly. Marfa Vseslavevna, the child's mother, had suspected that her son would be a chosen one, and these signs seemed to confirm it. She remembered the way she had conceived him, while being held captive by a terrible dragon. She had thrown a stone at him, but the reptile, instead of escaping, had twisted itself around Marfa's leg, and when she had managed to get it off her, she had realised that she was pregnant. In the end, the hero Dobrynya Nikitich had saved her, and she had gone back home, but her son had been conceived with a snake, so she expected him to possess special abilities that normal children lacked.

Within an hour and a half after his birth, little Volkh turned to his mother, and to her astonishment, he spoke to her: "Mother, don't wrap me in a soft cloth, but let me wear a shining armour! Let me wield a mace or a spear worthy of a hero!" As much as Marfa expected some prodigy, she was not prepared for such a thing, so she trembled with fear. "What strange being are you, that you can already speak? Will you become a sorcerer? Will you shed people's blood?" she sighed. The little boy did not answer, and his mother started taking care of him. When he was seven years old, she entrusted him to a teacher to learn how to read and write, and Volkh proved to be an outstanding pupil, mastering several languages and learning everything with ease. By the time he was ten years old, he had already mastered several spells, being able to transform himself into a hawk, flying high in the skies, into a wolf with grey fur, being able to run through the woods faster than anyone else, and into a large pike, able to swim in the deepest seas. Thanks to these three animal forms, Volkh had power over the realms of the heavens, the earth, and the waters. He was only twelve years old when he began to gather numerous warriors around him. Although he was still very young, he had tremendous charisma, and his extraordinary abilities made him great in the eyes of others, who therefore wished to follow him.

One day, when Volkh was fifteen years old, he heard rumours about the king of India (or the sultan of Turkey, in other variants) and his plans to invade his lands. He immediately ordered his army to intercept the enemy and protect his homeland, but such a regiment of men needed large supplies. While they were camped at the edge of a forest, Volkh ordered the soldiers to prepare nets and traps for wild animals, or to go hunting with bow and arrows in order to procure excellent meat. The men went into the forest for a few days, but when they returned, their hands were as empty as their bellies. One night, after everyone had gone to sleep hungry and demoralised, Volkh secretly wandered off into the deep forest and turned into a wolf. Alone he caught many beasts and drove many more into the traps prepared by his comrades. The following day, the army discovered that all the animals they had failed to catch had miraculously been trapped that night, and they were happy to feast. Soon, however, the men began to get tired of eating red meat; they craved some fowl meat as well. Volkh then advised them to prepare nets to hang among the highest branches to catch some birds, but several days passed without any success. Once again, it was up to the hero, this time in the shape of a hawk, to lead the birds into the traps, and he did the same later, in the shape of a pike, scaring the fish into the nets of his men. Thanks to him, nobody went hungry, and they all reached the enemy kingdom well-fed and in high spirits.

Once there, they realised that they could not go unnoticed, since the territory was swarming with guards. Thus, Volkh left his companions and flew to-

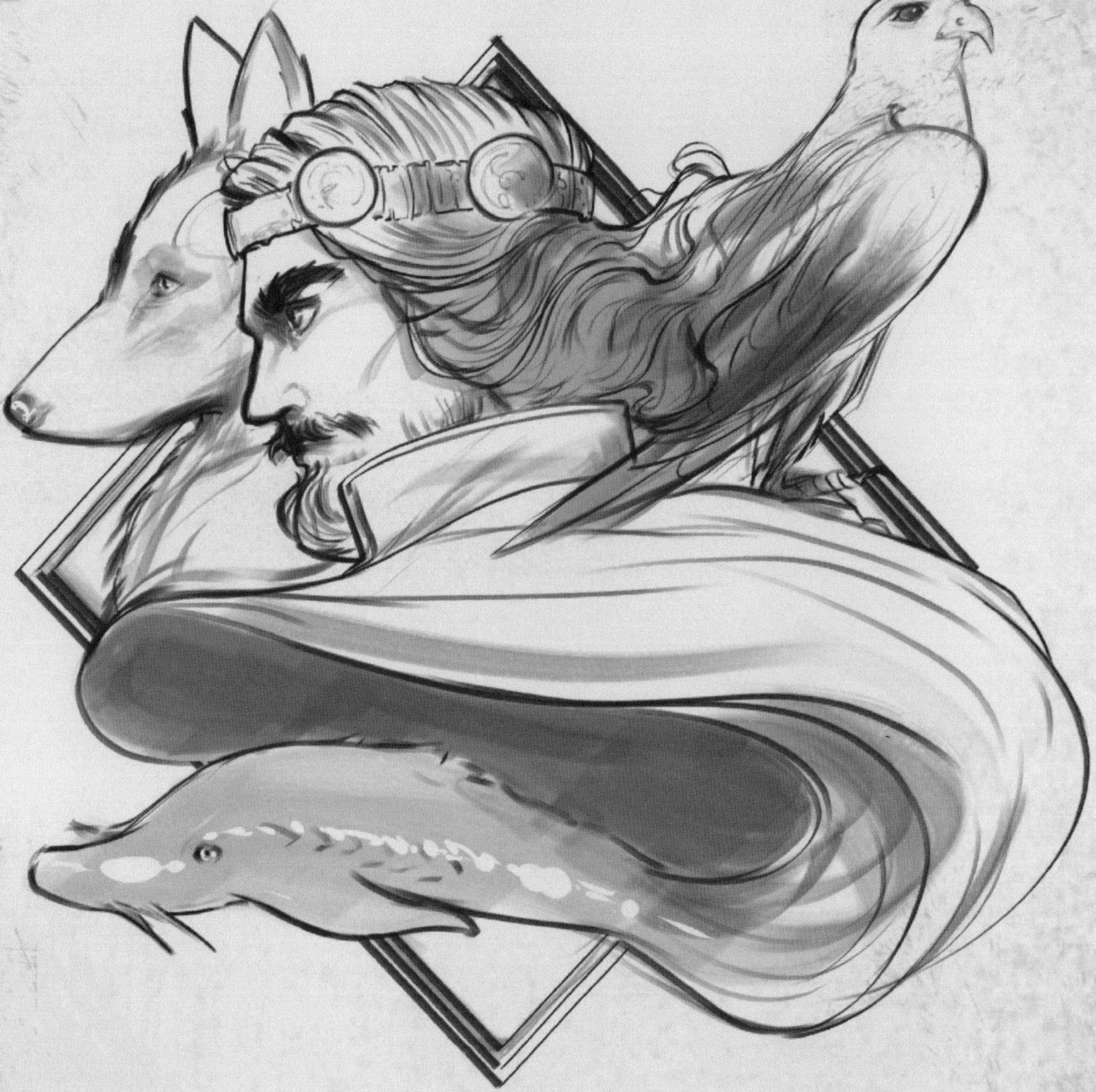

wards the palace in the form of a falcon. Once inside, he assumed the appearance of a swift ermine, sneaking between the feet of the guards and searching the armoury. As he slipped from one hiding place to another, he overheard a conversation between the ruler and his wife. "A mighty enemy is at our gates! – said the queen – Last night I had a premonitory dream: a small white bird fought against a large crow and defeated it, scattering its black feathers to the four winds. That crow was you, my lord! Brace yourself; command your troops to take up arms!" Volkh, still in ermine form, realised he had little time left to act undisturbed before the soldiers prepared for battle. He slipped into the armoury, where he gnawed at the strings of the bows, scattered the gunpowder and removed it from the guns, then buried and concealed the smaller weapons and created as much havoc as he could. On top of this, he reached the stables, where he turned into a wolf and scared the horses away, then soared through the air like a majestic hawk, flying back to his army. He intended to lead them into the heart of the enemy kingdom, but he realised that they would soon be spotted and intercepted by the sentinels, so he had to act with greater secrecy. Using his powers, he turned his soldiers into ants, so that they could pass unseen through the walls of the enemy palace; here, they resumed their human appearance and slaughtered their enemies. After the victory, they divided up the loot, and Volkh took the queen, who had foreseen his arrival, as his wife.

THE TALE OF IGOR'S CAMPAIGN

The Slovo o pŭlku Igorevě *is an epic poem of extraordinary importance to better understand the Slavic deities. Indeed, it is the only source in which the gods appear in an epic context, rather than in a sermon aimed at condemning the belief in them. Their presence, combined with shamanic themes and elements related to the forces of nature, described as alive and endowed with a sentient spirit of their own, takes the style of this text back to the beginnings of Slavic paganism. Nevertheless, it is not devoid of Christian elements, since it recounts events that took place in 1186 that the poet probably experienced first-hand, given the vivid way he describes them. In any case, this text from the Eastern-Slavic Middle Ages retains an important link with the pre-Christian tradition and thus can help contextualise the Slavic deities.*

The poem begins by stating that it narrates events in a simple style, different from the rich style used by the storyteller and soothsayer Bojan, nephew of the god Veles, patron of poets, who used to wander with his mind like a shaman, among the branches of the great world tree, travelling as a bird or as a wolf, to bring back ancient knowledge. The strings of his *gusli* (a musical instrument similar to the Finnish *kantele* or psaltery) moved on their own as he sang his songs. The poem then recounts the deeds of Jaroslav the Wise, great prince of Kiev, and of his brother Mstislav the Brave, who fought with his bare hands against the prince of the Circassians. Jaroslav was an excellent ruler and favoured peace among the nobles. In contrast, Roman the Fair, supported and ill-advised by his brother Oleg, rebelled, allying with the Polovtsians and turning against his kin. These two brothers first brought the Polovtsians into the Russian territories, using them as allied troops, but the Polovtsians soon switched sides, attacking those who had favoured them. These Turkish people killed Roman and mercilessly razed and plundered Russia. It was a time of political strife, and the country found itself in the grip of various factions led by rival princes, as well as under enemy pressure.

Igor, the protagonist of this story, was Oleg's grandson, and due to his predecessor's bad political choices, as well as his own recklessness, he found himself fighting against the Polovtsians. In secret, ignoring the directives of his father Svyatoslav, the prince of Kiev, who had tried in every way to make peace with his enemies, Igor had decided to make an incursion into the Polovtsian territories. His brother Vsevolod, his son Vladimir, and his young nephew Svjatoslav, who was only nineteen years old, agreed to join the expedition. They intended to leave at dawn, and Igor had assembled his most loyal men, those who formed his *družina* (personal retinue), but just as he was about to set out, a black shadow darkened the sun. The soldiers looked up in dismay, looking at the ill-omened eclipse, but Igor was impatient to leave and urged his men: "Be brave! Let us face our enemies and gallop with steadfast hearts to the lands of the Don, whose crystal-clear waters will quench our thirst after the battle!" So the warriors stopped staring at the sky with its shadowy omen and set off, but they should have heeded that fatal warning. To those who could discern the weavings of fate, those soldiers would have appeared not as a glittering host of heroes, but as a flock of black crows bearing dark tidings, intent on a mad and dishevelled flight towards the Don.

Along the way, they were reached by the impetuous Vsevolod, Igor's brother, who led a troop of men determined to join the expedition. Once again, their path was paved with gloomy omens: the sun gave way to darkness, while stormy winds arose. Birds were screeching madly and the howls of wild beasts echoed across the steppe. The stone effigies of the ancient gods seemed to utter dark warnings as they grimly watched the passage of those hosts. Nevertheless, they never stopped marching in the dead of night; the wheels of their chariots whined like mournful swans, and the fog began to thicken. Finally, Igor's people reached the enemies and slaughtered them. The expedition was successful, and the princes raided the lands of the Polovtsians, obtaining a large booty and taking with them the most beautiful maidens they could find. Once the raid was over, they set off, scornfully using the cloaks and clothes they had stolen from their enemies to cross some treacherous marshes. When they stopped for the night, they could not imagine that vengeance would descend upon them like a flock of hungry crows. At dawn, a blood-red sky greeted them, while black clouds thundered in the distance. The winds, grandchildren of the god Stribog, blew impetuously, while the cries of the enemies resounded across the steppe. There were many of them, and they came from all directions. Soon Igor and his men found themselves surrounded, and the battle began. Vsevolod fought like a bull, slamming dozens of enemies to the ground, and Igor backed him up, slashing at them for three days before dropping his insignia to the bloody ground. Due to Oleg's actions, hatred had been kindled among the Russians, the descendants of the god Dazhbog, and the country was in tragic conditions. Instead of the peasants singing as they worked the land, one would rather hear the cawing of crows feasting on corpses. Obida, the mournful swan-winged maiden, shook her white-feathered wings, thus banishing the times of plenty, while the princes fought in their greed, and foreigners took advantage of that disorganisation to attack Russia.

Igor was taken prisoner, and that same night his father, Prince Svyatoslav, had a terrible nightmare. His body lay on a bed made of yew wood, a poisonous plant connected to the realm of the dead, while wine mixed with sorrow was prepared for him, and his enemies dropped a pearl on his corpse. When he woke up, he heard what had happened to his two sons Igor and Vsevolod, who, like daring hawks, had fled from their native nest only to be defeated by their enemies, and he could hardly hold back his tears. Moreover, his nephews had also been captured. With great effort, Svyatoslav had managed to make peace with the Polovtsians, but his sons' expedition had rekindled the fires of war that the prince had tried to extinguish. "Why, my sons, did you do this to your old father? – he exclaimed – Why did you act dishonourably, disregarding treaties and suddenly attacking the Polovtsians? Their vengeance was terrible, you deserved it". The prince grieved, knowing full well that the Polovtsians would certainly not stop after defeating Igor; they would raze other Russian cities, and now the elderly Svyatoslav could not count on his brave sons to defend them. He called upon the great warriors who had once acquired great glory, as if their spirits could somehow offer protection. He recalled the exploits of Vseslav, the prince of Polock, who wished to conquer the city of Kyiv with the same ardour of a man in love. Vseslav waged war for a long time against the sons of the wise Jaroslav, and it was said that by day he ruled his kingdom, but by night he wandered through the moors in the form of a wolf, along the way of the great Chors (the Sun or the Moon). Vseslav was a sorcerer, and his actions against Kyiv were only one example among many fights between the Russians and the Polovtsians. While the elderly Svyatoslav regretted his sons' daring and foolish act, the beautiful Jaroslavna, Igor's young wife, also mourned his passing, weeping and wishing to assume the form of a seagull, to fly to the body of her beloved and be able to wash his blood-covered wounds. "Wind! – she lamented – Why did you guide the enemy arrows to my Igor? River Dnepr, take me the body of my husband, and you, shining Sun, why did you direct your rays against the men of Kyiv? You tired and weakened them with your heat!" Meanwhile, on the battlefield, the sky was filled with whirlwinds of light, and the northern lights swirled in the sky, as if a god was showing Igor the way back to the land of his ancestors. He was not dead, as his people feared, but the Polovtsians had taken him prisoner. One of his enemies, called Vlur, took pity on him and decided to help him escape. He waited until midnight and then whistled for the horses, inviting Igor to ride away while it was still dark.

The two galloped as far as the steeds could carry them; they were as swift as wolves or hawks, and they found shelter among the rocks with the agility of an ermine. Exhausted, they stopped at last by the river Donec, and Igor turned to the waters, saying: "River, you will be remembered for cradling this prince in your gentle waves, for offering him welcoming shores to rest on, for watching over him like a duck sleeping on the waters!" The river then replied: "Not so kind was the river Stugna, which swallowed up and swept away Prince Rostislav, the son of your brother Vsevolod." At that moment, they heard the cawing of crows, and Igor leapt up at once. That noise had in fact come from two Polovtsian commanders, Gzak and Končak, who were lurching among the reeds to search for the fugitive. They had followed him, and now that he had stopped by the river, they had a chance to hit him with their arrows. "If he dares to cross the river, I'll kill him", whispered Gzak. "We still have his son Vladimir. If Igor returns to Kyiv, escaping our arrows, we can make a deal, uniting young Vladimir and my daughter in marriage so that hostilities will cease," replied the other with far more wisdom. Igor actually managed to ford the river and return to Kyiv, which in his absence had fallen into a state of torpor, like a body deprived of its head. The sun shone on the prince and everyone in the city celebrated his unexpected reappearance. A few years later, Prince Vladimir also returned, together with his Polovtsian wife and their child. This marriage did bring some stability, but not for long. Soon, both Russians and Polovtsians would face a new enemy that would defeat them both. These were the Mongol armies of Genghis Khan, who would seize Kyiv and hold it for a long time.

DOBRYNYA NIKITICH AND THE KNIGHTS-ERRANT

Russian byliny *often feature the* bogatyri, *heroes based on historical figures. More precisely, they are the knights gathered around the historical figure of Vladimir the Great, Grand Prince of Kyiv around the year 1000. The* bogatyri *fought monsters and the enemies of Russia and, just like the Knights of the Round Table, they were brave and skilful warrior, always ready to rescue a maiden in distress and to protect villages from the attack of giants or dragons. Dobrynya Nikitich is one of the most famous heroes, based on the historical character of the same name, the maternal uncle and guardian of Grand Prince Vladimir.*

During a feast with his best knights, Prince Vladimir complained that he had yet to find a wife. The Lithuanian princess seemed to be perfect for him, but her father was not particularly impressed with Vladimir and did not consider him a good match for his daughter. Thus, Dunai Ivanovich stood up resolutely and said: "My sovereign, let me go all the way to Lithuania and convince the foreign regent to grant you the hand of the princess. I will not fail you!" Vladimir appreciated his offer and asked Dunai to take four hundred soldiers and large amounts of gold with him, to impress the foreign regent, but the knight refused. "The only things I need are a letter asking for the maiden's hand, healthy horses with new bridles and saddles, and a good travelling companion, such as my dear friend Dobrynya Nikitich". The prince granted him everything he asked, and the two *bogatyri* left Kyiv on their way to Lithuania.

When they arrived there, Dobrynya took charge of looking after the horses, while Dunai went to talk to the ruler. However, the king did not appreciate this visit, and after reading the letter Vladimir wrote, he called the guards. "Does that prince think he is worthy of my child? Nonsense! Moreover, why does he want the hand of my youngest daughter, and not the eldest? This is an insult, so his knight will go straight to the dungeon!" The soldiers drew their weapons

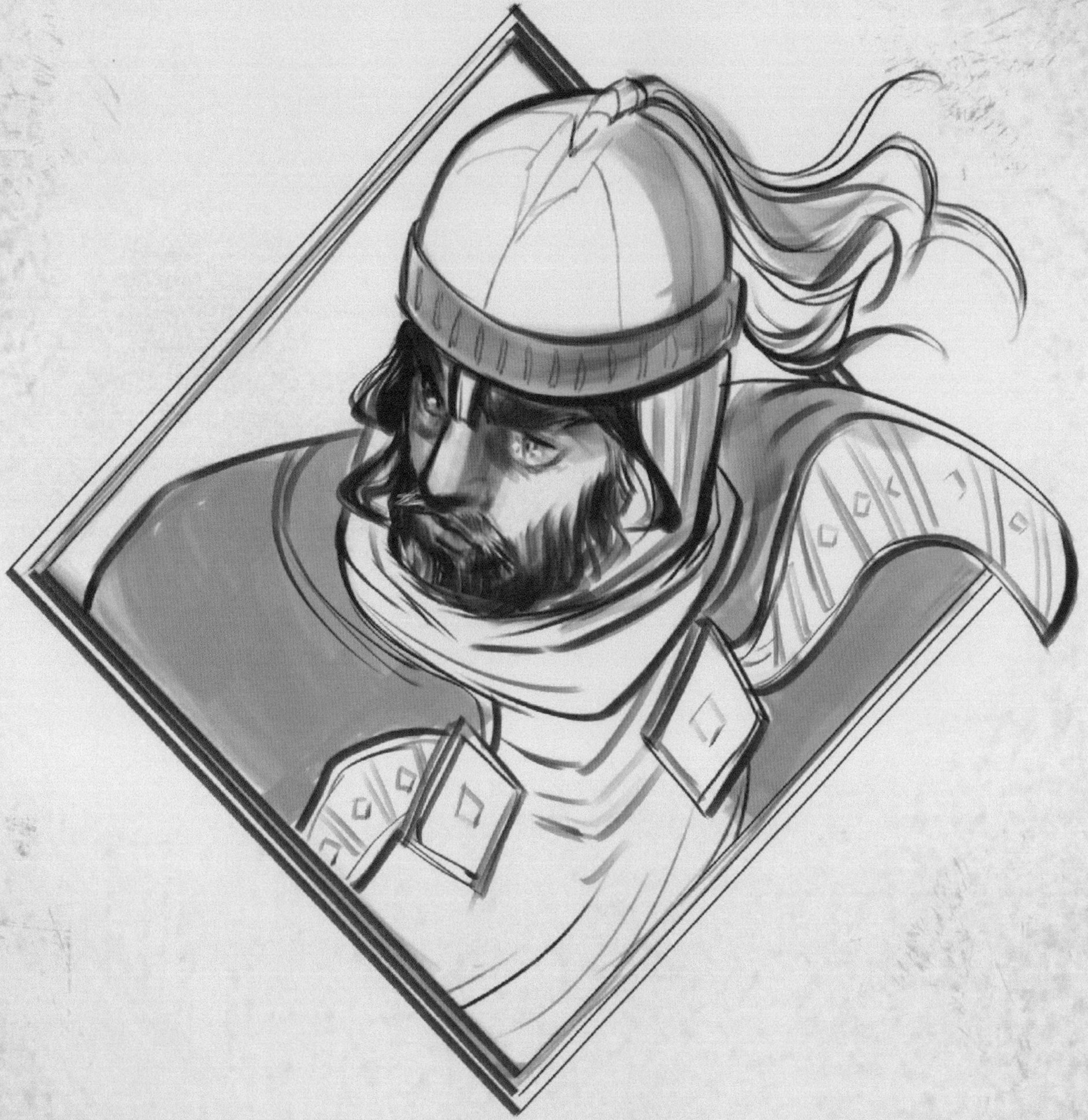

and attacked poor Dunai, while those stationed outside the palace tried to capture Dobrynya as well. Dunai drew his sword and tried to defend himself, but the guards were too many and soon pinned him down, ready to drag him away. At that point, though, the palace doors swung open, and Dobrynya appeared, with weapons dripping with enemy blood and a grim expression painted on his face. He demanded that his comrade be released, and the princess handed over to Vladimir. The Lithuanian king had no choice but to accept these conditions, so the two knights set off with Evpraksiya, the young princess.

That night, as they were resting near a campfire, they heard strange noises and noticed a shadow lurking in the darkness. "Someone is following us – whispered Dunai to his companion. – Keep your sword handy tonight". Despite the presence of that mysterious pursuer, the three slept until dawn without interruption. "There's something wrong with this whole matter, – Dunai muttered – and I don't want to see the princess in danger. Dobrynya, set off with her towards Kyiv, and I'll stay behind to find out who's after us and catch them when they least expect it". The *bogatyri* then parted ways, Dobrynya and the maiden riding away while Dunai waited in secret. Soon the spy came, riding after the princess and unaware that someone was watching him in turn. Dunai charged him with such force that he unsaddled him, but as the spy hit the ground, his helmet rolled away, revealing a cascade of golden hair. Hiding underneath the armour was a beautiful maiden. "I am Evpraksiya's elder sister, but I prefer fighting and riding over embroidering and combing my hair. You took my little sister away by force and I intended to get her back, but you caught me, and now my plan has failed," she explained as Dunai helped her to her feet. He had to admit that he was impressed by the girl's courage and beauty, so he proposed to her; that way, she would not have to part with her beloved sister.

When the two couples reached Kyiv, a double wedding took place, uniting both Vladimir with Evpraksiya and Dunai with her sister. The latter enjoyed the company of the *bogatyri*; she declared that Alyosha Popovich was the best at sword fighting, but that nobody was more skilled in archery than her. Dunai was deeply offended, as his wife did not think him valiant enough, so he challenged her: "I will show you how good an archer I am! We'll put a silver ring on each of our heads, and the other will have to shoot an arrow through it. Are you ready? You'll try first!" Perhaps he hoped that such a difficult and dangerous challenge would intimidate her, but the *polyanitsa* (as the female *bogatyri* are called) accepted without even flinching. She took an arrow and aimed, then shot it right through the middle of the ring, without even making it vibrate. Not satisfied, she shot two more arrows and succeeded three times in a row. Then, with a triumphant expression, asked her husband if he had had enough. "All right, you're very skilful, – he said, his pride crushed – but that doesn't mean that I can't beat you. Now it's my turn; get ready!" For the first time in her life, the *polyanitsa* was afraid, and begged Dunai to reconsider: "You know your aim isn't like mine. It's too dangerous; you'll end up killing me!" The knight, however, did not listen to her and prepared his bow, even though his arm was shaking. His wife was right, but he could not show his weakness. "Don't do this! – she sobbed – Think of the child I'm carrying! He'll be a special child, different from all others; his limbs will be gold and silver, his hair will be adorned with splendid pearls, and his eyes will sparkle with the light of the sun and the stars!" Dunai paid no heed to that nonsense meant only to discourage him, and he shot his arrow. As expected, he missed the target, and his wife fell to the ground, dead. She was really pregnant after all, and the child she was expecting, when taken from her womb, had all the wonderful features she had described. Dunai, overcome with grief, felt he had no other choice: he pitched his spear into the ground and hurled himself upon it, perishing just like his wife and child whom he had killed in an excess of pride.

Meanwhile, after handing the princess over to Vladimir, Dobrynya had resumed his travels. One day, he found the lair of a dragon, where a baby dragon waited helplessly for the return of its fierce, gigantic mother. That region was plagued by a terrible reptile that devoured the livestock and set the villages ablaze. The nights often glowed with fires, and the pillars of smoke tinged the dawn with the colours of despair. That little creature would become a voracious scourge

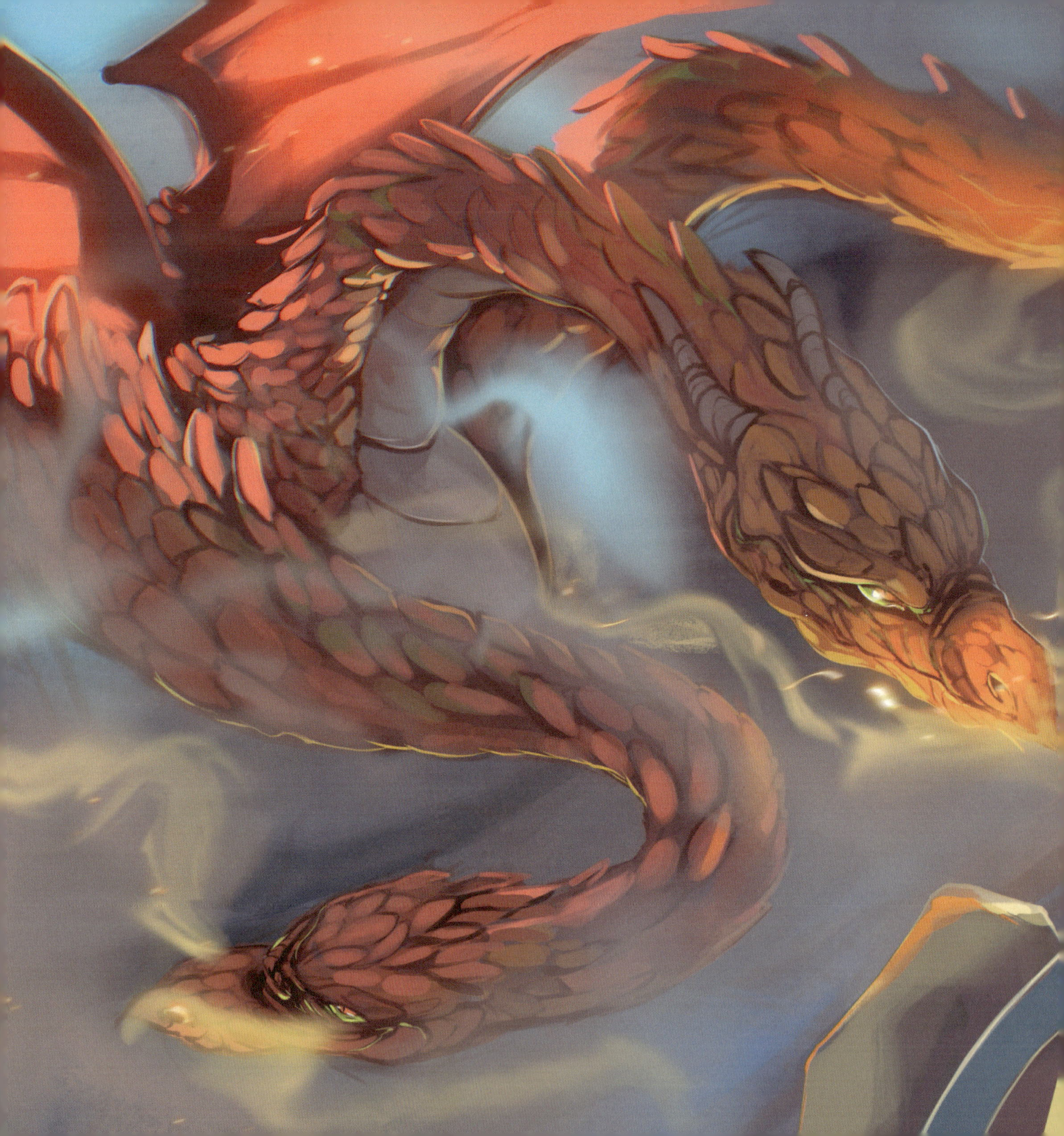

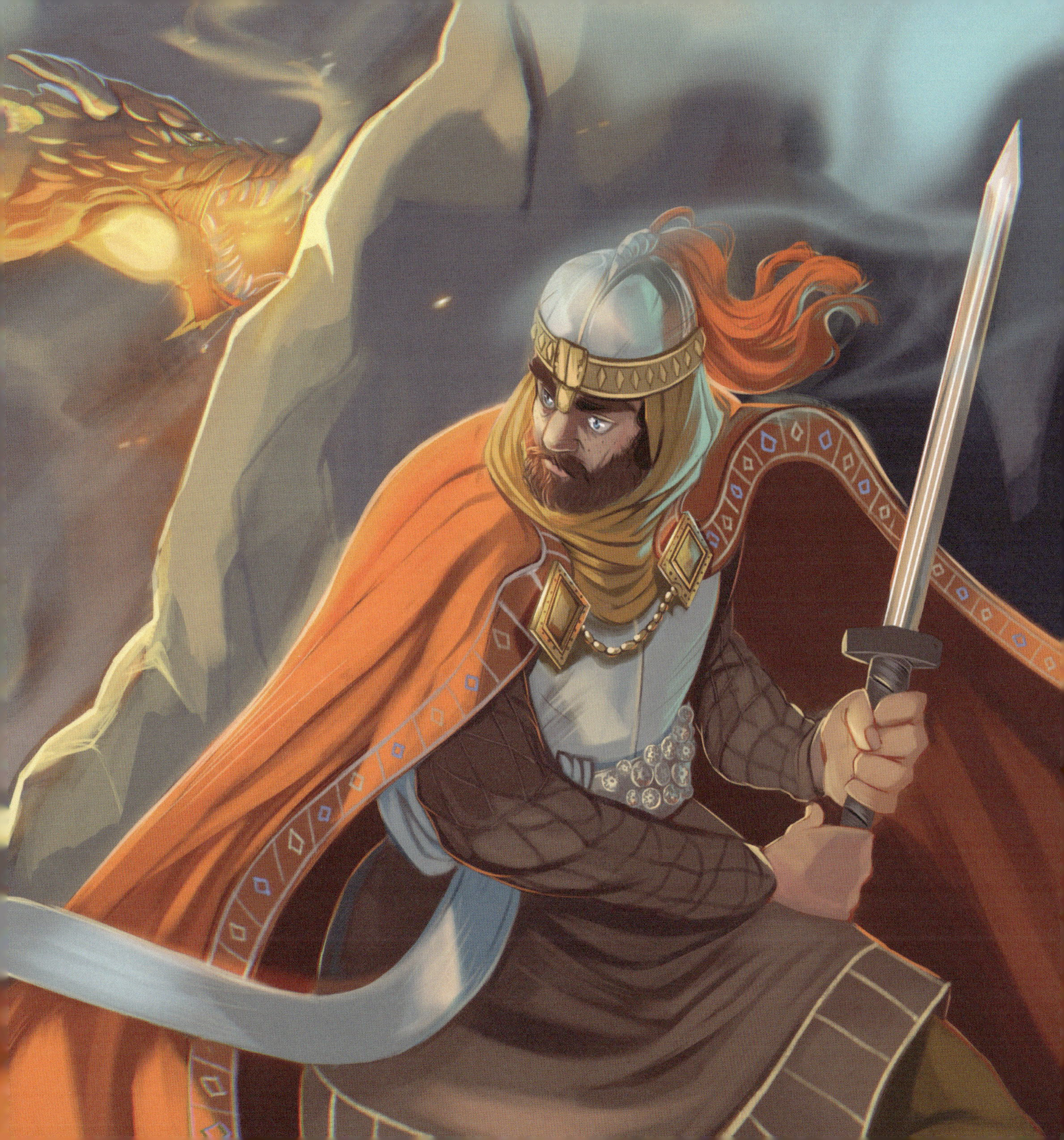

for the poor people, and Dobrynya knew it, so he killed it mercilessly and went back to his land, without waiting for its mother to return. When he was home, he recounted what he had done and learnt that those lands were haunted by the fearsome Zmey Gorynych, a female dragon with twelve ravenous heads. "She surely knows you killed her baby, – his mother told him – and if she finds you, she will destroy you. Please, my son, never return to those regions! Stay away from the dragon's vengeance!" But Dobrynya was not afraid of Zmey Gorynych. On the contrary, he was curious to meet her and fight her, so he did not follow his mother's advice and went back to those lands.

The sun was high in the sky, and the knight had travelled a long way, so when he saw the river Puchai, he tied his horse to a tree and took off his weapons and clothes, swimming and washing himself. As he refreshed himself, he felt the ground tremble while tall pillars of smoke rose from the forest. As the dragon's twelve heads roared in unison, Dobrynya kept his composure and dived into the water, swimming as fast as he could towards the shore. The monster was approaching from the side where the hero had left his weapons and mount, so he had to swim to the opposite bank, where he arrived completely unarmed. The dragon approached, ready to take her revenge, but Dobrynya noticed a strange hat on the ground. He knew that that kind of hat was worn by pilgrims travelling to the monastery on Mount Athos and was therefore a holy object. He grabbed it, since it was the only object available nearby, and hurled it forcefully at the dragon, making it spin like a circular blade. The hat was indeed full of holy energy, for it managed to cut off some of the dragon's heads. Zmey Gorynych ended up on the ground and begged the bogatyr to spare her. "I have learnt my lesson, but now let me live. I promise to no longer raid, devour sheep and children, or set villages on fire. You must, however, promise never to set foot in these lands again". Dobrynya was naked and unarmed, so he thought it wise to accept that deal. As he went back to retrieve his clothes and armour, he discovered that his black horse Voroneyushka, Little Raven, had fled when the dragon approached threateningly. Thus, he had to walk back to Kyiv for many days.

Even from afar, he could see black smoke rising from the city, as if many buildings were burning. He rushed to Vladimir's palace and found the ruler in despair. A many-headed dragon had attacked the city, spitting fire and flames, destroying many houses, and finally carrying off his niece, Princess Zabava. Dobrynya sighed. "So Zmey Gorynych did not keep her word!" he exclaimed, thus revealing his connection to the dragon. "So you know that monster! – said Vladimir – I command you to find him and bring me back my niece!" The hero had vowed not to set foot in the dragon's lands again, but the prince would not listen. "Zabava's life is all that matters now! If you refuse to save her, I will have your head cut off!" The bogatyr was forced to obey, so he returned to his mother to prepare for his departure. He was disheartened, for he would never have wanted to break his word; moreover, he no longer had a horse that could lead him quickly to the dragon's lair. His mother then pointed out to him the old horse that had belonged to his father, which was grazing peacefully, covered in mud and dust. It did not look like a valiant mount to Dobrynya, but he had no choice, so he cleaned him up and saddled him, finding that he was not so bad once he had taken care of him. His mother then handed him the silk whip his father used to spur the horse. "Just touch him with it, and he will immediately regain all his vigour", she explained. The hero rode off, marvelling at the swiftness of the horse, and soon he reached the mountains where the dragon dwelt.

Zmey Gorynych was not in the cave, but the den was teeming with tiny baby dragons, which Dobrynya crushed under the hooves of his mount before they could grow as large and cruel as their mother. However, one of the baby dragons managed to bite the leg of the steed, which began to limp, but a gentle touch of the silken whip was enough to bring it back to full strength, and thankfully so, for at that moment, amidst black swirls of smoke, the dragon returned. She found Dobrynya, her old enemy, and saw what had become of her spawn. "How dare you? – she roared with her many heads – Not only did you kill my babies, but you even broke your promise! You are a noble knight of Kyiv, I never expected this!" The bogatyr replied that it was the dragon who had broken the pact first, attacking the city and taking Zabava away, but this excuse did not seem to have any effect. "Of course I did not keep my word, I am a dragon! It was you who had to keep it, you foolish hero full of silly ideals about honesty and valour, but I see you were quick to forget them. If you came all this way to claim the princess back, know that you have come a long way for nothing, for you will never get her back!" These words set Dobrynya's aflame. He drew his sword and attacked the ferocious monster, and the battle between the two continued for three long days, but in the end the bogatyr triumphed, exhausted, in the middle of a literal lake of blood. The blood that gushed from the dragon's wounds was so copious that it had trapped the hero, but Dobrynya prayed to Mother Earth, asking for her help, and immediately a rift opened in the ground, draining off the whole scarlet lake. Now that the lair was clear, the knight was able to explore it and look for the prisoners, discovering that there were more than expected. Among them was Marfa, the mother of Volkh Vseslavevich, and in the last cave he finally found Zabava. He went back to Kyiv victorious, returning to Vladimir his beloved niece.

The perfect ending to this story would be a marriage, but Dobrynya did not have noble blood and so he could not marry a princess. Saddened because he could not take a wife despite his epic deeds, he was advised by his mother: "By now it's clear that there is no suitable girl for you in Kyiv, so go and find her beyond the borders!" The hero accepted her suggestion and once again mounted the steed he had learnt to appreciate. As he rode across the steppe at full speed, he noticed that there was a second rider. He mounted a horse with a shiny black coat and was equally fast. Dobrynya did not know this warrior and wanted to test his strength by shooting an arrow straight at his helmet. His shot was precise, but the arrow bounced off the hard metal while the other continued to advance without even taking notice. The bogatyr then shot a second arrow, a third, and finally managed to unsaddle his opponent. As he approached to see who it was, he discovered that it was a *polyanitsa*, an indomitable warrior girl who did not stay helplessly on the ground, but got up at once, drawing her sword and threatening Dobrynya. "Who are you, and how dare you knock me out of my saddle? If you're older than me, I will kill you, but if you're younger, I will appreciate your courage and regard you as a brother". The hero did not like her hostile words, so he refused to answer, and grabbed his weapon instead. Before they could fight, a bizarre thing happened: the horse with the night-black coat reared up and spoke: "I recognised this knight who does not wish to reveal his name. He is Dobrynya Nikitich, and he is the same age as you, Natasya!" The *polyanitsa* weighed the situation for a few moments, then lowered her sword. "You are neither older nor younger than me. Since we are the same age, we shall get married." Since the bogatyr had set off just to find a wife, he gladly accepted her proposal, pleased to have found a strong and courageous bride.

He took her to Kyiv and, for a certain time, they were happy, but one day Vladimir gathered his most trusted knights, explaining that the Lithuanian king, their ally since he had married his youngest daughter, had been attacked and had asked for help. "Which of you will lead my armies to aid Lithuania?" he asked at last. Alyosha Popovich stood up, but not to volunteer. "I think the most suitable is Dobrynya Nikitich. It was he, indeed, who brought the daughter of the Lithuanian king here and started this alliance" he stated. Vladimir fully agreed, but not so Dobrynya, who was nevertheless forced to obey the prince's orders. Before leaving, he bid farewell to his bride, who promised to wait for him for twelve years, before taking another husband. "I hope to return much sooner – said the hero with a sigh – but if not, marry an honest man who will take care of you. I only ask that you don't marry Alyosha Popovich..." "Why? – she asked – Perhaps you fear he sent you to war on purpose, to get rid of you so she could marry me?" Dobrynya laughed it off: "Of course not, Alyosha and I are like brothers, he would never do that. He proposed me because he thinks I am the most valiant!" After bidding farewell to his mother and wife, the hero left, but the war in Lithuania went on longer than expected and kept him away for more than twelve years.

In Kyiv, many times did Alyosha Popovich claim that Dobrynya had died, but Natasya did not want to believe it and continued to wait for him, as she had promised. However, when the twelve years were up, she felt she had kept her vow, so she agreed to remarry. It was Alyosha Popovich who courted her more than anyone else. Natasya finally agreed, because Alyosha was handsome and brave, and by now she had made her peace with Dobrynya's death. The bogatyr was sleeping in his tent before yet another day of gruelling fights, when a strange flapping of wings awoke him. Two doves had entered his tent, but not by accident. The birds were in fact able to speak and wanted to warn him of the impending marriage between Alyosha and Natasya. Indignant because his best friend had betrayed him, and because his wife was breaking her promise, Dobrynya mounted his saddle and rode back to Kyiv. His years at the border had deeply scarred him, and he now looked like a scruffy old man. Thus, he pretended to be a wandering minstrel, and no one recognised him, allowing him to attend the wedding banquet to sing his stories. So moving were the verses of this mysterious poet from afar that the bride wished to favour him by personally bringing him a cup of mead. According to custom, the minstrel could now return the favour, so he took a second cup and offered it to the beautiful bride, but before leaving it in her hands, he let his wedding ring fall in it. When Natasya had emptied the cup, she noticed the ring and recognised it as Dobrynya's. Looking closer at the old minstrel, she noticed the similarities with the husband she had thought dead, and so she threw herself at his feet, sobbing and asking for forgiveness. The hero told her to get up, for it was not her fault; someone had deceived her, bringing her false news of his death. Alyosha paled as Dobrynya drew her sword. "Forgive me, brother! I have done wrong, but I'm sure that an honourable and just knight like yourself will be able to grant forgiveness..." Those words slid over the bogatyr, who grabbed his rival by the neck and dragged him to the ground, ready to skewer him on the floor of his own wedding feast. He would have done so if Ilya Muromets, one of Kyiv's noblest knights, had not stepped in, stopping his hand and persuading him to prove his greatness even in forgiving. All the guests stared at him in silence, full of tension, especially Prince Vladimir, who would not have appreciated bloodshed among his knights. Finally, Dobrynya sheathed his weapon, but showed no respect for Alyosha; in fact, he never spoke to him again. However, he did forgive Natasya's wrong, and the two became closer than ever.

ALYOSHA POPOVICH AND TUGARIN SON OF THE DRAGON

Alyosha was considered one of the most valiant and charming bogatyri, *although he did not always behave according to a code of honour. He was an inveterate playboy; he lied and cheated, yet he is one of the most famous knights of Kyiv, on par with Dobrynya Nikitich and Ilya Muromets. He, too, may be a fictional version of a historical figure, Alexander Popovich of Rostov. Popovich means "Son of the Pope", but the term Pope is also used to describe high prelates, not necessarily the Pontiff. It is said that his father was a bishop named Leontius, and historically we find a bishop with this name who was killed during a pagan revolt.*

Alyosha was born and raised in Rostov. When he felt ready, he chose to go to Kyiv, to the court of Prince Vladimir, where he hoped to begin a new and honourable career, staying away from women and wine, which had too often gotten him into trouble. When he arrived in the great hall, instead of taking his place at the table with the other knights, as he was invited to do, Alyosha preferred to sit in the shadows, next to the stove like the beggars and servants, where he could carefully observe the hall and its occupants.

One day, as they were eating and chatting merrily, a loud noise made the diners gasp. The doors had suddenly swung open, and a monstrous giant had made his entrance. He was as tall and sturdy as an oak; he had wide, fierce eyes and long ears. He was Tugarin Zmeyvich, the son of the dragon, a giant who bore the name of a Polovtsian *khan*, reflecting the battle between the civilised forces of Kyiv and the nomadic and savage forces of their enemies. Tugarin did not show the slightest respect for the prince; indeed, without asking permission, he sat in the place of honour, right between Vladimir and his bride. Petrified, the guests just stared at him, and only Alyosha dared to joke: "The prince and his wife must have had a very serious fight, if they allow such an ugly beast to separate them!" Tugarin paid no heed to the chatter coming from the servants' area, and plunged his own knife into a succulent swan, which he took all to himself,

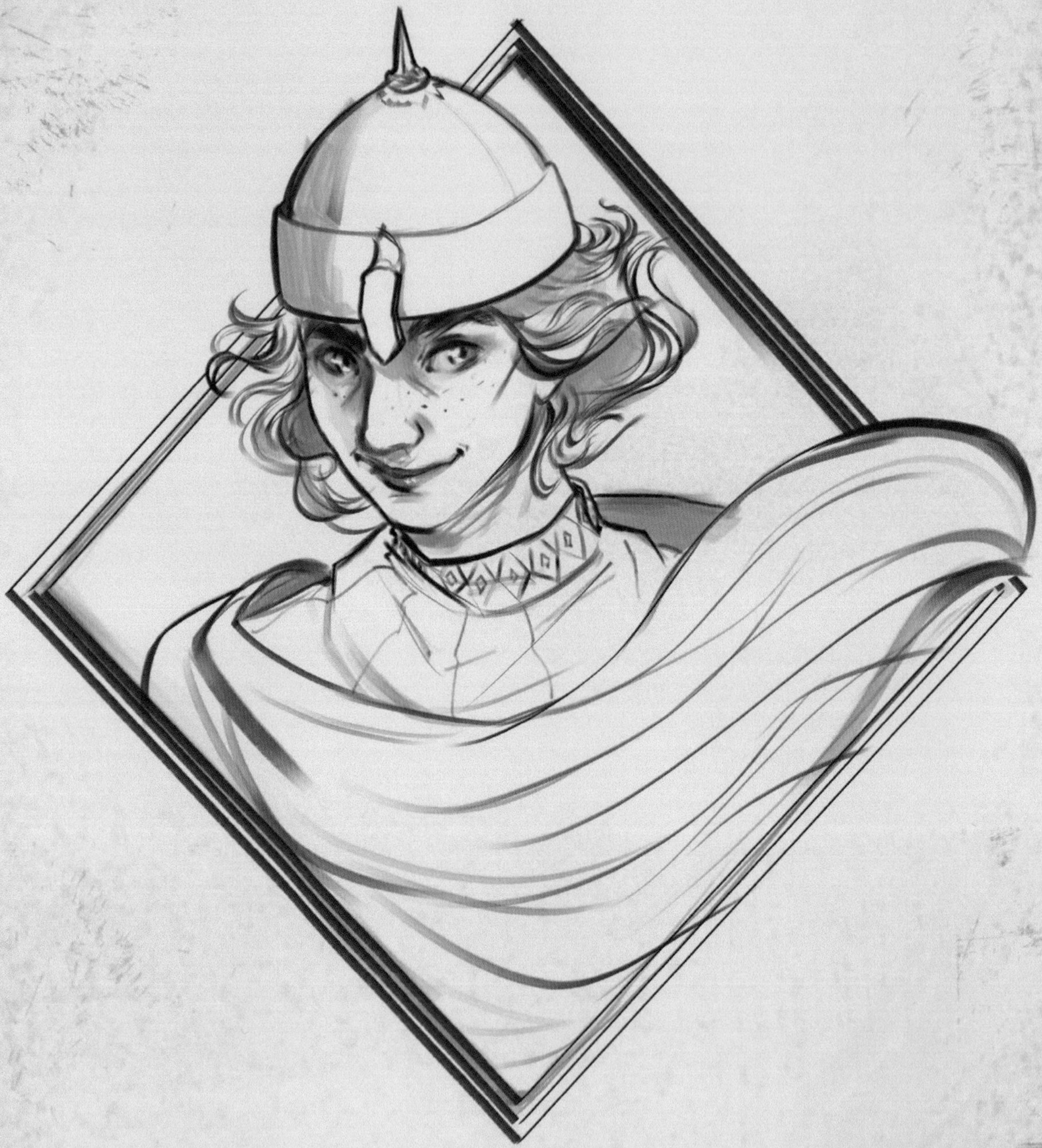

devouring it in a few disgusting bites. Once again, no one had the courage to oppose him, and only Alyosha spoke, in an amused tone: "My father used to have a ravenous dog that would dive into the food just like that big guy does. One day it tried to devour an entire swan and choked on a bone. Let's hope the same happens now, so that we get rid of such a rude guest!" Tugarin was too busy chewing noisily and paid no attention to the arrogant poor man who had spoken; instead, he emptied an entire barrel of mead with one greedy gulp. Alyosha did not miss the new chance to remark: "I once had a cow who drank with such eagerness that she seemed to be dying of thirst. Eventually, she choked and died due to her own voracity. Maybe we'll be lucky enough to see something like that again tonight".

At that point, Tugarin became nervous and hurled his knife straight at the one who was mocking him. Alyosha's squire, however, caught it and deferentially handed it over to his lord. The giant had not expected this, and he realised that the man must not be a common beggar. "Who are you?" he asked with a grunt. "I am Alyosha Popovich, – the hero replied, stepping forward – and I bet you've heard of me before. You should have thought twice before giving me your knife! It's perfect for cutting out your heart! It will be really humiliating for you to be killed by your own weapon". Tugarin could no longer bear those insults. "Shut up! Tomorrow, on the steppe, we'll see who laughs last. I challenge you to a duel!" Alyosha accepted, and the next day he went to the agreed place, but he did not do so in his knightly guise. Instead, he disguised himself as a pilgrim with a tunic and a wooden staff. There, he waited for his adversary, who arrived late but in a very scenic manner. Tugarin indeed came gliding through the air with two majestic wings that he had not had the night before. Alyosha found this very strange and observed them carefully, noticing that they were made of paper. He then prayed to the heavens for some rain, and his wish was granted. Large drops fell on the paper wings, making them so heavy that they broke and caused Tugarin to crash to the ground. At that point, Alyosha finished him off with a blow of his staff right to the head. For this bold and cunning action, he is regarded as one of the most famous and courageous *bogatyri*.

MIKULA, THE EXTRAORDINARY FARMER

Mikula is a bogatyr that started as a farmer, dedicated to the land and agriculture. He was favoured by Mother Earth, who granted him unrivalled strength. His figure may have ancient origins related to the underground god and protector of herds, Veles.

Volga Sviatoslavovich, the nephew of Prince Vladimir of Kyiv, was travelling through the countryside to collect taxes, when he heard a cheerful whistling sound. A peasant was at work, and he could hear him ploughing the soil, while the beasts uttered their cries around him. Volga decided to approach him to collect the tribute, but although he felt the farmer was close, he could not reach him, even if he spurred the horses to a run, while the other was busy working. Finally, after two and a half days of riding, the man appeared in the distance. The farmer was humming as he ploughed and sowed, followed by his animals. Whenever he came across an obstacle, such as a large log or a boulder, he would simply lift it up and throw it to one side, as if it were weightless. The man's plough was made of gold and silver, and the farmer himself wore elegant and precious clothes. Volga grew increasingly curious and approached to ask him who he was. "I'm Mikula Selyaninovich, – he replied cheerfully – and I see that you're travelling with bags full of money. Be careful because there are bandits around here. They have their base near the river and rob anyone trying to cross the bridge. The other day they tried it with me too, but I routed them all in no time".

Volga was impressed by the man's strength and asked him to accompany him across the river, to show him safely where the brigands were, trying to avoid them, or to help in the fight if needed. Mikula willingly agreed and followed Volga, but soon he looked back, concerned. "My plough! I left it in the middle of the field, where anyone could steal it. It's quite precious, and I'd like to hide it first." Volga nodded, unwilling to waste any more time. "Don't worry; I will

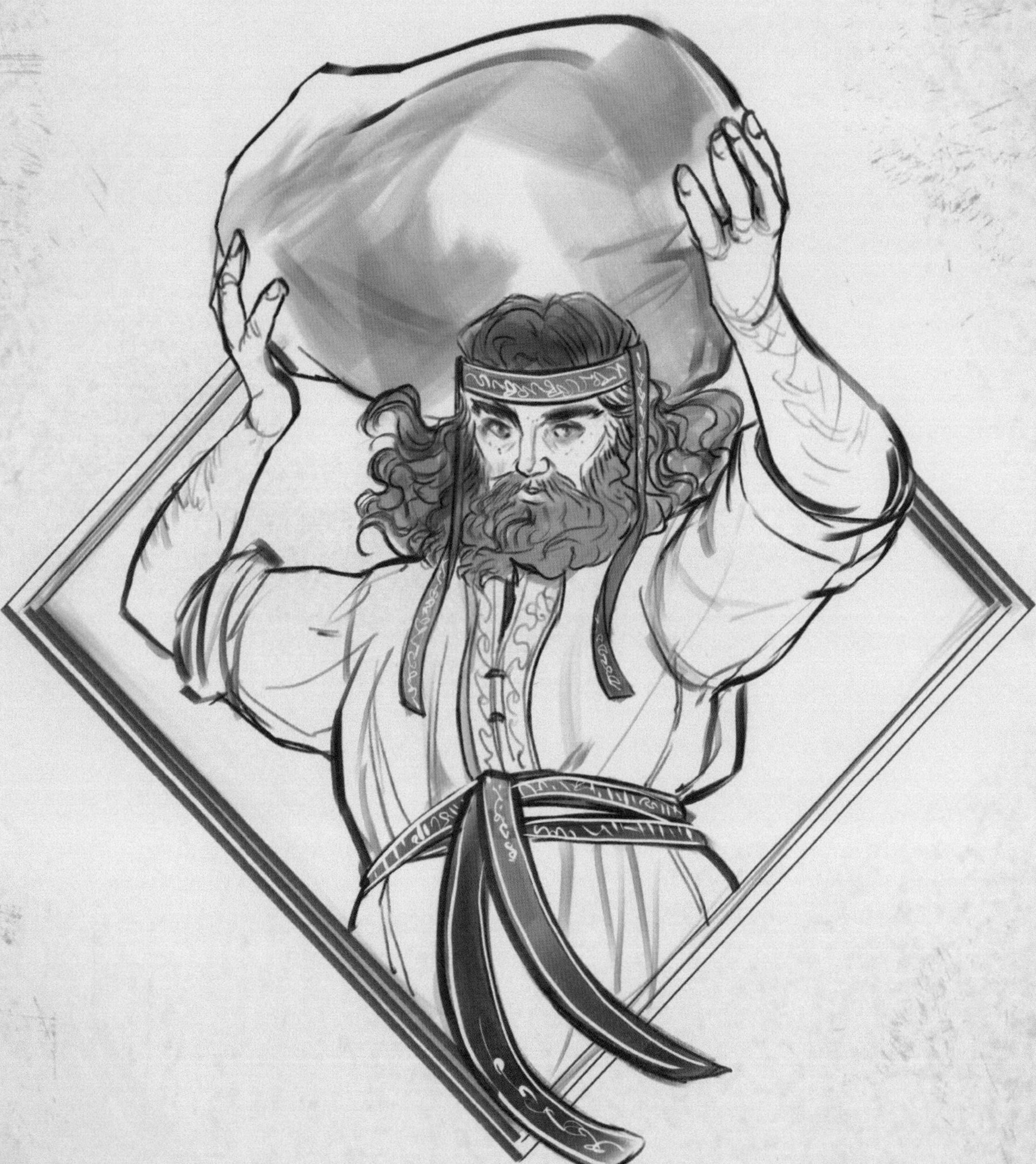

send five of my best men to secure it". The soldiers obeyed, but even working together, they could not move the plough one inch. When they came back empty-handed, Volga sent the whole army to move the plough, but still they were unsuccessful. Finally, seeing them in trouble, Mikula reached his tool and hid it in the bushes by lifting it with one hand. The prince's nephew was so impressed by Mikula's strength and genuine goodness that he wanted him by his side, giving him titles and land and making him a bogatyr.

ILYA MUROMETS AND THE LAST GIANT

Ilya Muromets is one of the most famous bogatyri, *but his figure is linked to the Orthodox saint Ilya Pechersky. Sviatogor is considered the last of the giants, a character connected to ancient paganism, who had to give way to new heroes such as the Knights of Kyiv.*

Ilya was born on a humble farm, and as a child he was so weak and sickly that he could barely move. When he was thirty-three, he was healed by a group of pilgrims, among whom, according to some legends, was Jesus Christ himself. "Now you are a strong man, and your heart is pure, so go and help the needy. But be very careful! Do not challenge the giant Sviatogor or the peasant Mikula, for their strength is extraordinary. Beware also of Volga Yaroslavich. Although it may seem easy to defeat him, his tricks can prove very dangerous", his healer advised him. At that point, Ilya decided to join the knights in the service of Vladimir of Kyiv. He set off, solemnly promising that he would not shed a single drop of blood until he had reached the Kiyv Cathedral, where he would attend Mass.

While riding, he noticed large war fires in the distance and heard the desperate screams of women and children. The city of Chernigov was under siege, and Ilya prayed to the Lord to forgive him, because he was going to break his vow

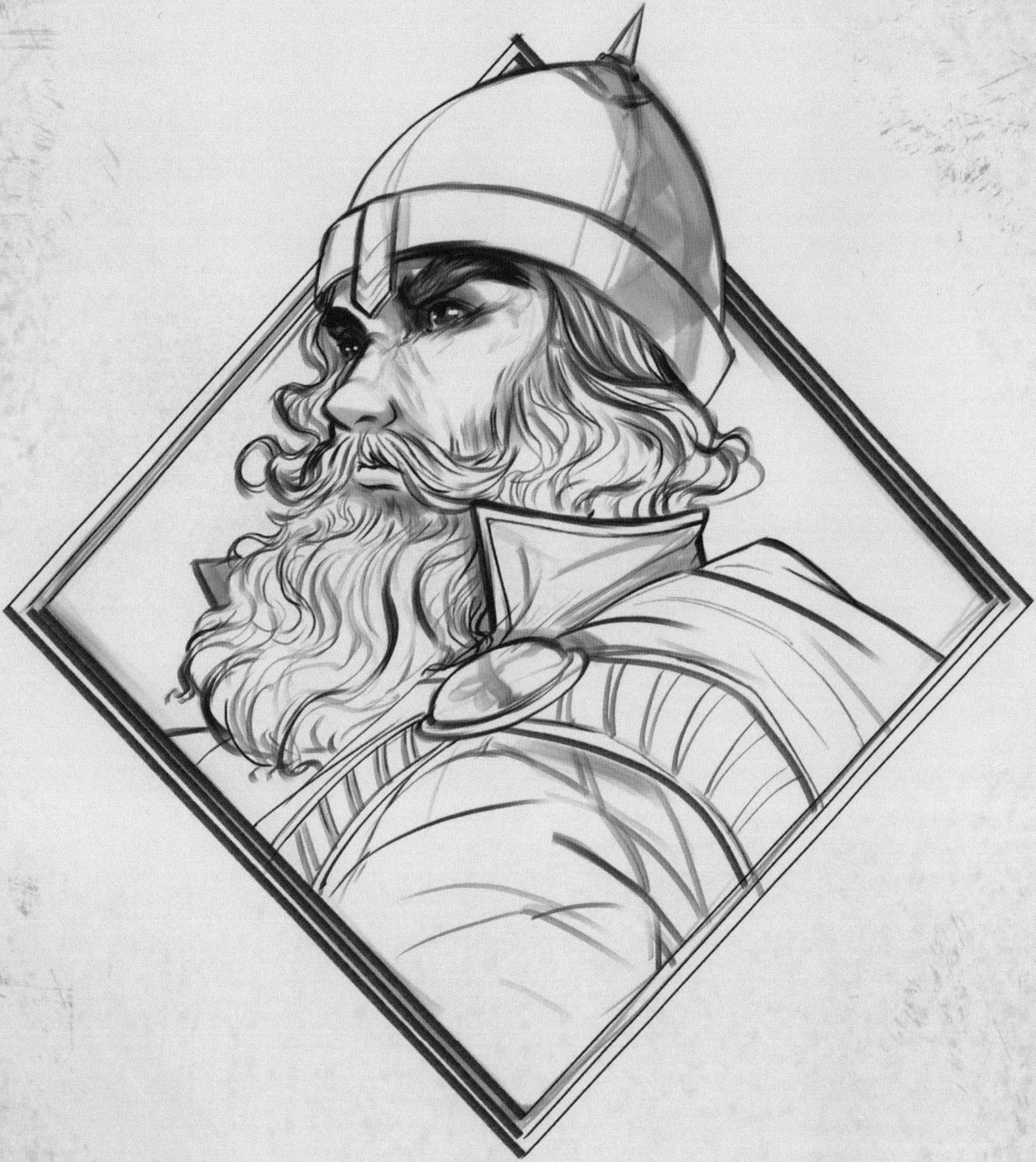

to help those innocent people. Alone, he routed the entire enemy army, and the citizens wanted to welcome him as a hero and offer grand festivities in his honour. Ilya refused, though, because he wanted to reach Kyiv on time for Mass and had already lost too much time. He inquired about the shortest route to his destination and was told that it passed through a ford guarded by the brigand Solovei Rakhmatich, known as the Nightingale because he was half human and half bird. It had been years since anyone had passed that way, because all those who had attempted to ford the river had never returned. Ilya, however, was not afraid; besides, he had to fulfil his vow, so he set off along the uneven and weedy path, since no one used it anymore.

When he reached the ford, he noticed a gigantic nest on top of seven large trees; it must have been the Nightingale's home. The bandit had noticed the rider and welcomed him with one of his powerful whistles, so loud that it shook the forest and made Ilya's horse bolt. Without losing concentration, the hero nocked an arrow and shot it at his enemy, who soon fell to the ground, wounded but still alive. Ilya quickly bound and gagged him, determined to take him to Vladimir to decide what to do with him. As he travelled with his prisoner, he came across a cottage, but its inhabitants did not seem inclined to welcome Ilya; on the contrary, they greeted him with axes and pitchforks. They were the Nightingale's relatives, determined to free him. The bandit knew that, in a head-on fight, his people would soon be annihilated, so he beckoned them to lower their weapons. "Don't harm this knight. He's the most valiant man I've ever met and deserves our respect. Rather, offer him a good hot meal and a place to rest tonight!" he said, persuading the family members to show friendliness. His plan was good, but Ilya knew that, once in the house, unarmed and maybe even asleep, he would be attacked by the Nightingale. Thus, he rejected their hospitality and killed them one by one. When he finally reached Kyiv, he found he was late for Mass, but still went to Prince Vladimir and showed him the famous outlaw he had captured. The prince examined him. "Are we sure he is really the Nightingale? I would like to hear one of his famous whistles". Ilya shook his head, because those sounds were too loud and very dangerous, but Vladimir insisted, so the hero asked his prisoner to emit a much weaker sound than usual. The Nightingale ignored those words and, bringing his fingers to his mouth, whistled as loudly as he could, a sound that killed all the palace guards at once and echoed through the entire city of Kyiv. Ilya then cut off his head upon Vladimir's order. He fed the human half of his body to the wolves and the bird-like half to the crows.

Afterwards, Ilya Muromets wandered through the wilderness again, looking for monsters to defeat and princesses to save. At last, he reached the slopes of the Holy Mountain, where he found a huge tent in the shade of a colossal oak. Ilya entered and was surprised to see a bed so large that more than ten men could have slept on it comfortably. Intrigued, he hid in the oak branches and waited for the mysterious owner to show up. Soon the earth began to shake, and a giant appeared on the horizon, advancing with heavy steps until he reached the tent and entered it. Ilya peeped in and saw that the giant was carrying a precious chest under his arm. Inside the tent, the giant put it on the ground, took out a key tied around his neck, and opened it to let out a beautiful maiden. The two dined together as husband and wife; then she asked to be allowed to take a walk, since she had been huddled in the chest for a long time. The giant let her go while he stretched out on the wide bed. The woman walked around the clearing, but when it was time to go back, she noticed the knight hiding in the foliage and asked him to come down. "Help me. The giant Sviatogor holds me prisoner! He forced me to marry him, and he keeps me locked up in that chest for fear that I might escape. Even when I try to escape, with a couple of quick leaps he always manages to catch me. Please set me free!" she said, taking him by the arm and pulling him into the tent, where Sviatogor was snoring loudly.

Ilya did not want to kill an opponent in his sleep, as it would not be honourable, and while he was thinking about how to deal with him, the colossus started yawning and rubbing his eyes. "He's waking up! Quick, hide! He'll kill me if he sees you!" the woman implored, urging Ilya to slip into one of the giant's large pockets. Crouching uncomfortably, the knight waited there until dawn. When

Sviatogor finally woke up, he put his wife in the chest and rode off. He mounted his horse and spurred him on, but the animal snorted and shook his head in annoyance. "I already have to carry you, who are no lightweight, and on top of that I have to bear the burden of that poor woman in the box, but this time you ask too much of me. I cannot carry you, her, and even a bogatyr!" Sviatogor, at that point, became suspicious and took his wife out of the chest, imagining that she had tried to betray him. Without a second thought, he cut off her head, and after having solved this problem, he rummaged through his clothes until he found Ilya Muromets. "I could have killed you last night, while you were asleep, – said the knight – but I did not, because I am an honourable person. I hope you will return the favour". Sviatogor appreciated those words and decided that he would not kill him. On the contrary, he asked him to get his steed and ride together to seek great adventures.

Ilya and the last giant travelled together until they found a huge stone sarcophagus. It was too large for the bogatyr, but it looked just the right size for Sviatogor. The giant lay down inside it and even tried to close the lid, although it did not seem like a good idea to Ilya. As soon as the coffin was sealed, he heard the giant's cries from inside: "Let me out! I can't open the lid from the inside!" The knight tried to move it, but it was too heavy for his human arms. "Use my sword for leverage!" suggested the giant, but even so, the lid did not move an inch. "Apparently, I'm going to die in here, – Sviatogor said, resigned, after several attempts to push the lid from the inside with all his might – after all, it looks like this sepulchre is tailored for me. Tie my horse nearby, so it can stay with me until the end" he requested. Ilya did so, and with a heavy heart he left the last of the giants behind, aware that his lineage would soon disappear forever.

Ilya Muromets served Prince Vladimir faithfully for many years, and when he felt his time had come, he found himself at a crossroads. Three paths opened before him. The sign on the first path read "Death", the sign on the second read "Marriage", and the one on the third "Wealth". At that point in his existence, Ilya thought it appropriate to take the first path. He advanced confidently until he reached the hideout of several brigands who tried to rob him. The hero defended himself, defeating all adversaries, and then discovered that the path ended there. He turned back, thinking that those bandits might have represented a quick death for many ordinary people, but not for him; thus, he carved new words on the sign, announcing that the danger had been eradicated and the road was now safe. Not knowing where else to go, he took the second street, until he found himself in front of a beautiful palace, where a young girl invited him to have lunch in her company. She proved lovely and affectionate, and eventually led him to her rooms. This seemed very suspicious to Ilya, so, when they were in front of the bed, he pushed the girl onto it, revealing a trap. The bed turned upside down, becoming a revolving trapdoor that plunged the woman into the dungeon below, imprisoning her and then spinning again to look like a regular bed. The knight searched for an entrance to the dungeon and discovered that the cruel maiden had seduced and captured dozens of knights. He freed them all and then returned to the crossroads, where he changed the second sign as well. Finally, he took the last road, which led him to a field in the middle of which towered an enormous boulder. Ilya lifted it and found an immense treasure hidden underneath. An old knight errant did not need all that wealth, so he distributed most of it among the poor and changed the words of the last sign. He had no choice but to return to Kyiv, where he used the last remaining treasures to commission the construction of a cathedral. They say that he carefully supervised the work and looked forward to seeing it completed. Finally, when the church was ready, Ilya realised that his life had found its glorious fulfilment. His body turned to stone, and that was the very last stone that was used to erect the Kyiv Cathedral.

According to another legend about Sviatogor, one day, the giant was riding his horse, when he was intrigued by a cheerful whistling sound coming from a traveller he could barely make out on the horizon. He spurred his steed on, determined to catch up with him, but the other always remained at the same distance, as if he were as fast as a galloping horse. Even more startled, Sviatogor shouted to attract the attention of the mysterious fellow, and the latter finally stopped and put down the sack he was carrying on his shoulders. "Who are you, and what are you carrying?" inquired the giant, and the other motioned for him to look in the bag himself. Sviatogor dismounted, tried to lift the bag, and found, to his utter dismay, that he could not. Sviatogor was a giant, and his strength was legendary; it had never happened that he could not lift something, and now that small bag was putting him to shame. Red and sweating from the effort, he had to give up at last. Once more, he asked the strange traveller who he was and why his bag was so heavy. "My name is Mikula, – replied the other with a smile – and in this bag I'm carrying the whole world, so don't be ashamed if you can't lift it". The giant stared at him in amazement. "If you can carry the earth itself on your back, it means your powers are extraordinary, so tell me what my fate will be!" Mikula shrugged. "I don't know, but I can tell you who can reveal it to you. Reach the Northern Mountains, and once there, under the tallest oak, you will find a blacksmith. Ask him the same question, and you will have your answer". The giant thanked him and left.

Soon, in the valleys of the Northern Mountains, he heard the unmistakable sound of a hammer beating on an anvil. Under the tallest tree he found the smith, just as Mikula had assured him, and as he approached, he noticed that he was carefully forging two hair-thin threads. "What are you doing?" he asked curiously. "I'm forging the fate of those destined to stay together," explained the craftsman, igniting the giant's curiosity even more. He then asked if his fate would also be intertwined with that of a maiden. "You won't like the answer," the blacksmith warned him, but Sviatogor insisted. "Well, your future wife is in a village on the seashore, but she lives on a mound of dung, and she's covered with it from head to toe," he revealed in the end, to the giant's dismay. He did not know whether to believe those words, so he went in search of the village by the sea, where he found that there really was a girl living in filth. Her skin was brown and crusted like the bark of a fir tree, so Sviatogor did not want to marry her. Full of disgust and pity, he drew his sword and stabbed her, making her fall to the ground, dead. Then, however, he regretted his act and left a purse full of gold at her feet in atonement.

After the giant had left, the maiden recovered from her wounds. The clean cut produced by Sviatogor had split the bark that surrounded her, and out of that foul-smelling envelope emerged the most beautiful creature that ever lived. She found the gold in the pouch and used it to start a business as a merchant, which proved very fruitful and allowed her to travel the world. Sometime later, Sviatogor heard of an extraordinary merchant who sold goods of the highest quality and whose beauty was divine. Curious to see her with his own eyes, he went to visit her, and was so enchanted that he started courting. After much effort, the maiden consented to marry him at last, and when they were now husband and wife, Sviatogor noticed the scar on her breast. "Because of a curse, I used to live alone, covered in bark and surrounded by filth. Someone, however, suddenly struck me, destroying the wrapping that imprisoned me and leaving me with a bag full of gold. I don't know who did it, but I would like to thank him with all my heart. My life has changed because of his deed". At that point, the giant told her everything, realising there was no way to escape destiny.

WHY THERE ARE NO MORE BOGATYRI IN RUSSIA

Seven of the most famous *bogatyri* decided to travel together. One of them was the furious Vasilii Buslayevich, Dobrynya's half-brother on his mother's side. Vasilii was extremely intelligent, but in his younger years he assembled a group of fighters only eager to raid, drink and party, and his mother could hardly keep his ambitions in check. The others were Godenko Bludovich, Vasilii Kazimirovich, Ivan Gostinyi Syn, the famous dragon slayer Dobrynya Nikitich, the daring Alyosha Popovich, and the devout Ilya Muromets. The seven heroes camped for the night on the banks of the river Safat, but in the morning, Dobrynya noticed a tent on the opposite bank. He stopped to observe, thus noticing that it belonged to a Tatar, one of the *bogatyri*'s bitter rivals. Dobrynya unsheathed his blade and challenged the infidel to a duel, and the latter did not hesitate, taking the field without fear and fighting with extraordinary ferocity. He managed to unsaddle Dobrynya and finish him off with a stroke of his scimitar before he could even get up.

By this time, the other *bogatyri* were ready to leave, but they found that one of them was missing. Alyosha Popovich went to look for Dobrynya, who was once his closest friend, but whom his unbridled love for beautiful women had driven away, and he found his corpse in the middle of the steppe. A little further on, the Tatar warrior was dismantling his tent, so Alyosha realised what must have happened. Screaming in rage and pain, he challenged the slayer of his comrade, who got ready for a second fight. The strokes thundered swiftly, and both men proved to be excellent fighters, inflicting wounds on their opponent and standing despite their own. Finally, Alyosha's despair prevailed, and in his rage, he slashed at the Tatar, leaving him stunned on the ground. "I'll kill you without mercy. I'll avenge Dobrynya!" he yelled, with blood in his eyes, but at that moment, a raven swooped down and landed beside the helpless body of the steppe dweller. "Spare him, – he cawed – and I'll give you the Water of Life and Death, with which you can bring your friend back to life". Alyosha would have liked to stick his weapon in his enemy's heart and seal his victory, but bringing Dobrynya back to life was more important, so he accepted the raven's bargain. The bird flew away and soon came back with a small vial of clear liquid. He poured it over Dobrynya's corpse, watching in amazement as he awoke from his stupor, returning to life, his wounds fully healed. The Tatar, meanwhile, had slipped away, but no one took any notice, for they were all busy witnessing the prodigy and hugging their dear friend again. They hardly had time to set off again before an immense cloud of dust rose in the distance. An army of Tatars was approaching, probably summoned by the enemy that Alyosha had spared at the raven's behest. The seven *bogatyri* mounted their trusty steeds and firmly gripped their swords and shields, ready to face this immense horde of infidels. Despite their obvious numerical inferiority, the heroes distinguished themselves, fighting as they had never fought before, keeping their minds on their homeland, and trying to defend it from the cruel invaders. Each of them faced and defeated at least a hundred opponents, fighting tirelessly for three hours and three minutes, until they realised that no enemy was left on the battlefield. At that point they laughed, feeling relieved, and gathered on the riverbank, washing their blood from the wounds and the enemies' blood from their weapons.

"We were incredible! No one will ever manage to equal our triumph!" exclaimed Alyosha, brushing off the dust from his clothes. The others agreed and began to congratulate each other. "I saw you beheading those Tatars as if you were reaping wheat with a sharp scythe! And you, Dobrynya, faced at least ten of them all at once! Not to mention how Ilya chased down the last remaining ones, preventing them from escaping and calling for more reinforcements!" In their pride, they felt truly unbeatable. "After this victory, I want to see who will dare to challenge us! We're more than mere mortals now!" Alyosha yelled, boisterous, unaware that two men had silently come up behind him. "We should be intimidated by your strength – said one of them – but we're eager to test you!" The *bogatyri* burst out laughing, exchanging a knowing look. "We have routed an entire army on our own. What's the hope of just two men against the seven greatest heroes of all time? Leave while you can!" they suggested, but the two remained convinced of their words. Alyosha stepped forward, "Friends, go ahead and cool off at the river. I can get rid of this annoyance on my own. I'll join you in a few seconds" he said, drawing his sword and pouncing on his opponents. With two swift slashes, he cut them in two exact halves; then, pretending to yawn because it had been a rather boring duel, he made his way back to the river. "Where are you going? We're still up!" he heard. Turning around, shocked, he realised that his enemies had become four. Dobrynya came to help, and in turn managed to knock all his opponents to the ground with large wounds in their chests. The two exchanged a glance. Since Alyosha had tried to take the other's wife, they had not spoken to each other, but now they were satisfied and turned their backs to the battlefield. Ilya, however, pointed at something behind them. "Where did those men come from? There were two of them, and now there are eight!" The entire group of *bogatyri* jumped into the fray, but for every enemy they knocked down, two more immediately sprang up, and soon they found themselves surrounded. For the first time in their heroic lives, they were afraid. "This time, we'd better run!" exclaimed Alyosha. Ilya noticed a cave in the mountain and pointed it out to his comrades, who quickly sought refuge in it. As soon as they entered the cave, they immediately turned to stone. Their pride had been punished and served as an example to all the other knights, who stopped feeling unbeatable and returned to living simple and moderate lives. This is why there are no more *bogatyri* in Russia.

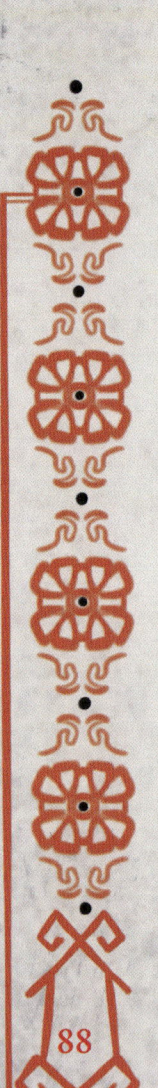

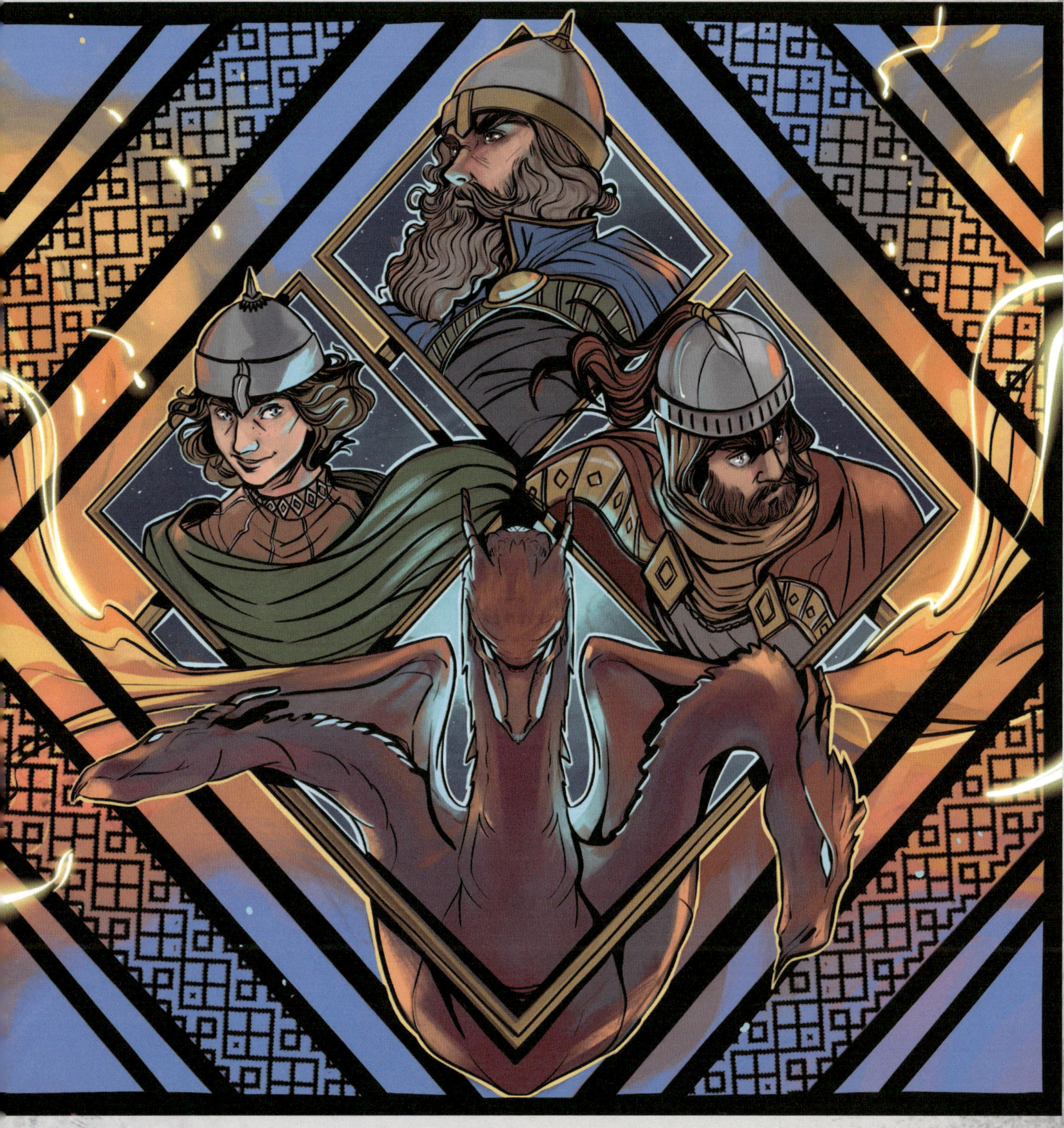

90

MYTHOLOGICAL CREATURES

MYTHOLOGICAL CREATURES

There are many spirits, legendary beings, and monsters in Slavic folklore, and a full list would soon become a whole encyclopaedia. Thus, this chapter will focus on creatures that appear in legends and tales.

KAPSIRKO AND THE VODIANOI

The vodianoi (or vodnik) is the lord of water spirits. His name comes from the term "voda", which means water. He lives in the depths of lakes and has green skin, covered in seaweed and lake plants. Sometimes he is benevolent towards those who do not disturb him, but his rage can prove deadly. Sometimes he takes human form and goes to the mainland, where he takes care of his livestock; in this case, it is easy to recognise him because his clothes are always wet, and he leaves watery footprints behind him. As soon as his clothes dry up, he must immediately return to the water, otherwise he will die. It is said that he collects the souls of drowned people in small bottles that he treats as treasures and proudly displays to others of his kind.

The farmer Kapsirko was caught stealing firewood from his master, but instead of being sentenced to exile, he received a strange proposal. "Since you think yourself so nimble and cunning that you can take my belongings, let us see if you can steal my horse, well protected in the stables, and kidnap my wife. If you succeed without being discovered, you will be spared; otherwise, I will send you to Siberia, where you will freeze and starve!" said the master. Kapsirko had no choice but to accept and sneak into his master's house. Luckily, he was good at sneaking, and he managed to elude the servants guarding the stable, as well as to take his master's wife away. He put her on a sleigh drawn by the magnificent steed he had just stolen and hurried away before being seen. He stopped to rest by a lake, and there, as he was rinsing his face and wondered about his incredible feat, the water rippled and out came a *vodianoi*, the lord of those depths, covered in seaweed and scales.

Kapsirko recoiled in fright, but the creature was not interested in him; rather, he looked longingly at the woman sitting on the sledge. "Hand her over to me, – he demanded with his deep voice – and in exchange, I will give you enough gold to fill your hat". Kapsirko cared nothing for his master's wife, and all those riches were tempting, so he agreed. While the *vodianoi* was taking the woman to his watery realm, on his way to get the gold, the scoundrel opened his hat and placed it on top of the sledge, hoping that the lake spirit would not notice the hole he had made in it, so that whatever was poured into the hat would end up in the sledge's bag instead. The *vodianoi* returned with the promised gold and began to pour it into the hat, noticing that it took longer than expected. Finally, however, he managed to make it overflow with gold, so the deal was done, and the two said goodbye. Now that he was rich, Kapsirko no longer needed to return to his master. After some time, however, it was the master who came looking for him, complimenting him on the cunning way he had taken his wife away, but begging him to return her. Kapsirko had to refuse, because he had now sold her to the *vodianoi*, but the lord begged him, offering him anything he wished in return. His proposal was now quite inviting to the scoundrel, so he accepted.

Figuring that the lake spirit would not easily give the woman back, he devised a plan. He went to the shore and began to wind ropes and make a fuss, until the *vodianoi*'s head emerged from the waters and asked him what he was doing. "I'm going to drain all the water from this basin, and then I will use these ropes to hang and dry all its inhabitants," he replied in a naïve tone. The lord of the water spirits rose in all his might. "I will not let you do that!" he thundered, making the lake gurgle. At that point, Kapsirko shrugged, dropping the rope he was coiling, "All right, if you want me to give up, all you have to do is return the woman I've given you". The *vodianoi* refused, at which point Kapsirko proposed a challenge in three trials. "Whoever wins will keep the woman. If you think you're much more powerful than me, you've got nothing to fear". The creature did not back down and asked what the first test would be. To begin, the two of them would have to stand on the bank of the lake, and from there emit a whistle so powerful that it would cause their opponent to fall into the water. The *vodianoi* went first, and he managed to cause such a commotion in the air that Kapsirko faltered. Only thanks to his extraordinary balance, and after bouncing several times on one leg, did he manage to stay on his feet. Then came his turn, and as he whistled, he tripped his opponent with a stick, making him plunge into the lake with a loud splash. When he came out, he gave no sign that he had noticed the trick, so they went on with the second round. "This time we'll see which one of us can run faster, but I think I'll win without any problems. Even my little nephew would be able to beat you!" Kapsirko mocked him, hurting his pride. "Really? Then let him compete in your place!" replied the *vodianoi*, not realising that he was playing into his rival's hands. Kapsirko cheerfully agreed and soon showed up with a hare in his arms. "Meet my nephew. Go ahead, get set, and we'll see who reaches the end of the lake first". The two started running, and of course the hare was soon far ahead. As the *vodianoi* came back, defeated and out of breath, Kapsirko took a second hare, identical to the first one, and placed it on the grass. "You're such a loser! Look at my nephew: he ran at breakneck speed, and still he isn't tired at all" he chuckled. The other, humiliated, impatiently asked what the latest challenge was. "It's very simple, – Kapsirko explained – it's a hand-to-hand fight. If you prefer, you can surrender right now, because it's clear that I'm going to win. Even my old grandfather could beat you". Once again, the *vodianoi* fell into the trap, proposing to let Kapsirko's grandfather fight in his place. "If you insist, I'll go and wake him up. You know, he's very old, and he's taking a nap right now", said the scoundrel. He then went into a cave and called loudly. The *vodianoi* waited at the cave entrance, ready to fight, but he was overtaken by a bear, enraged at being awakened from his hibernation. Battered and irritated, the water spirit realised he had lost all three trials, so he handed over the woman before facing other humiliations, and then he hurriedly sank into the lake's depths. Kapsirko, gloating over his victory through cunning, returned the wife to his master, and received titles, lands, and riches that let him live in luxury until the end of his days.

MARKO KRALJEVICH AND THE VILE

The vile are nymphs linked to natural elements: water nymphs are called povodne vile *in Serbo-Croatian, air nymphs are called* zračne vile, *and forest nymphs are called* pozemne vile. *They love to ride on the backs of horses or deer, dance in circles in the forest clearings, and go hunting. They are benevolent, blessing those who are worthy with their healing powers, but their wrath can be destructive. They can take the form of hawks, wolves, swans, horses, or even whirlwinds, and each has a favourite warrior of whom they are believed to be the* posestrima, *the blood sister, helping him in times of trouble. In their connection to a particular hero, they resemble the Valkyries. The most famous* vila *is Ravijojla, the* posestrima *of Marko Kraljevich, an important figure in Serbian epic poetry, protagonist of numerous legends known among the Southern Slavs. There are many legends concerning his exploits, but here we will focus on those involving the vile. Marko Kraljevich is a hero modelled on a historical figure, Marko Mrnjavčevich, a Serbian and Macedonian king who lived in the 14th century.*

When Queen Jevrosima was pregnant, a mysterious seer came to speak to her and asked whether she would prefer her son to become a king or a hero. The woman promptly replied: "A king, despite his importance, is often hated by his people. Instead, I wish my child to be loved by all, becoming a hero ready to fight to help the innocents!" The seer then told her to immerse her newborn child in the waters of nine different springs and to have him suckled three times by a *vila*. The queen nodded but wondered how she was going to find one of the shy wood nymphs. She did not have time to ask the seer, because the lady had disappeared into thin air, revealing her supernatural nature and making Jevrosima believe that she was, in fact, a *vila*. When the child was born, he was named Marko, known to all as Marko Kraljevich, or Son of the King. The queen did everything the nymph had suggested, and soon her son became exceptionally strong thanks to those special treatments.

When he was old enough to ride, it seemed to him that all the steeds he was offered were too weak, and he proved this by grabbing them by the tail and lifting them off the ground. One day, while wandering through the woods in search of a horse worthy of him, he found a dark, wounded animal neighing in despair. Moved to pity, he took care of it and helped it to recover, thanks to the suggestions of a mysterious and beautiful maiden. When the horse had healed, the maiden, who was indeed a *vila*, invited Marko to wash the animal's coat carefully, and so the hero found that it was not completely dark but had white spots as well. "Now you are healed, so go back to your family!" said the prince kindly, urging the horse towards the forest. The animal, however, did not move, but stretched its muzzle gently towards the one he considered his trusted champion. "Why don't you mount him?" suggested the *vila*, but Marko shook his head, "Not even the king's sturdiest horses could bear my weight, so how could this one, when it has just recovered from serious injuries?" The nymph invited him to give the animal a chance, so Marko tried to lift it by the tail, discovering that it was as sturdy as a mountain. With joy, he mounted on its back and found that it was the perfect steed for him. "At last, I have found you! Your name shall be Šarac, the Spotted, and we shall be inseparable. I will share everything with you, even the wine that will be offered to me!" he said, stroking his black-and-white spotted coat.

Now that he had a noble steed, Marko was ready to become a hero in the emperor's service. He had many adventures and gathered a group of warriors, among whom was Milosh Obilich. One day, the two friends stopped to rest under a tree after a long ride, and Marko decided to take a nap. "Milosh, my friend, sing with your beautiful voice to soothe my sleep," he asked, but to his surprise, the other refused. "I'm sorry, but I cannot sing near this mountain. Here lives the *vila* Ravijojla, a beautiful blond-haired nymph, and unfortunately, one evening, when I was drunk, I started singing around here, and you can imagine how out of tune and annoying I was. I must have bothered her, because she appeared in all her fury, swearing that she would kill me if I dared to sing in her lands again". Marko comforted him: "Sing without fear. If Ravijojla shows up, I'll take care of her!" Milosh trusted his valiant friend and entertained him with the sound of his voice, but soon the *vila* heard him singing and grew indignant at his disobedience. Floating in the air, she shot a white arrow straight through the hero's heart. His ballad ended abruptly in a desperate gurgle, and Marko sprang to his feet, just in time to see a whirlwind in the distance. Without a second thought, he mounted his trusty Šarac and urged him to run with all his might. "They say that only the vile can heal the wounds they have inflicted. Run, Šarac, we must reach Ravijojla before Milosh leaves us forever!" He was oppressed by guilt, but his piebald was faster than any other steed, and they soon reached the *vila*, who was running as fast as the wind. Marko struck her with his war club, knocking her to the ground, then tied her up and led her back to his dying friend. As soon as Ravijojla woke up, the prince ordered her to heal Milosh, and she had to obey, for Marko had proved stronger than she was. She gathered some healing herbs and spread an ointment on the warrior's chest, healing the arrow wound. "Forgive me, Marko, for hurting your friend. From now on, I will be like a blood sister to you, and I will help you whenever you need it!" she said, thus gaining the perpetual friendship of the hero, who freed her and considered her like a sister.

Sometime later, Marko Kraljevich's adventures led him to clash with Musa, an outlaw of Albanian origin, who was said to be as proud and wild as the mountains of his homeland. The two faced each other, Marko with his scimitar made of Damascus steel, and Musa with a similar weapon, forged by the same craftsman. The two started exchanging blows, and for a moment the hero thought he had won, for he had pierced the heart of his rival; but still the latter continued to fight, as if nothing had happened. Finally, the Albanian hero managed to push Marko down onto the grass, and then sat on his chest, pinning him down tri-

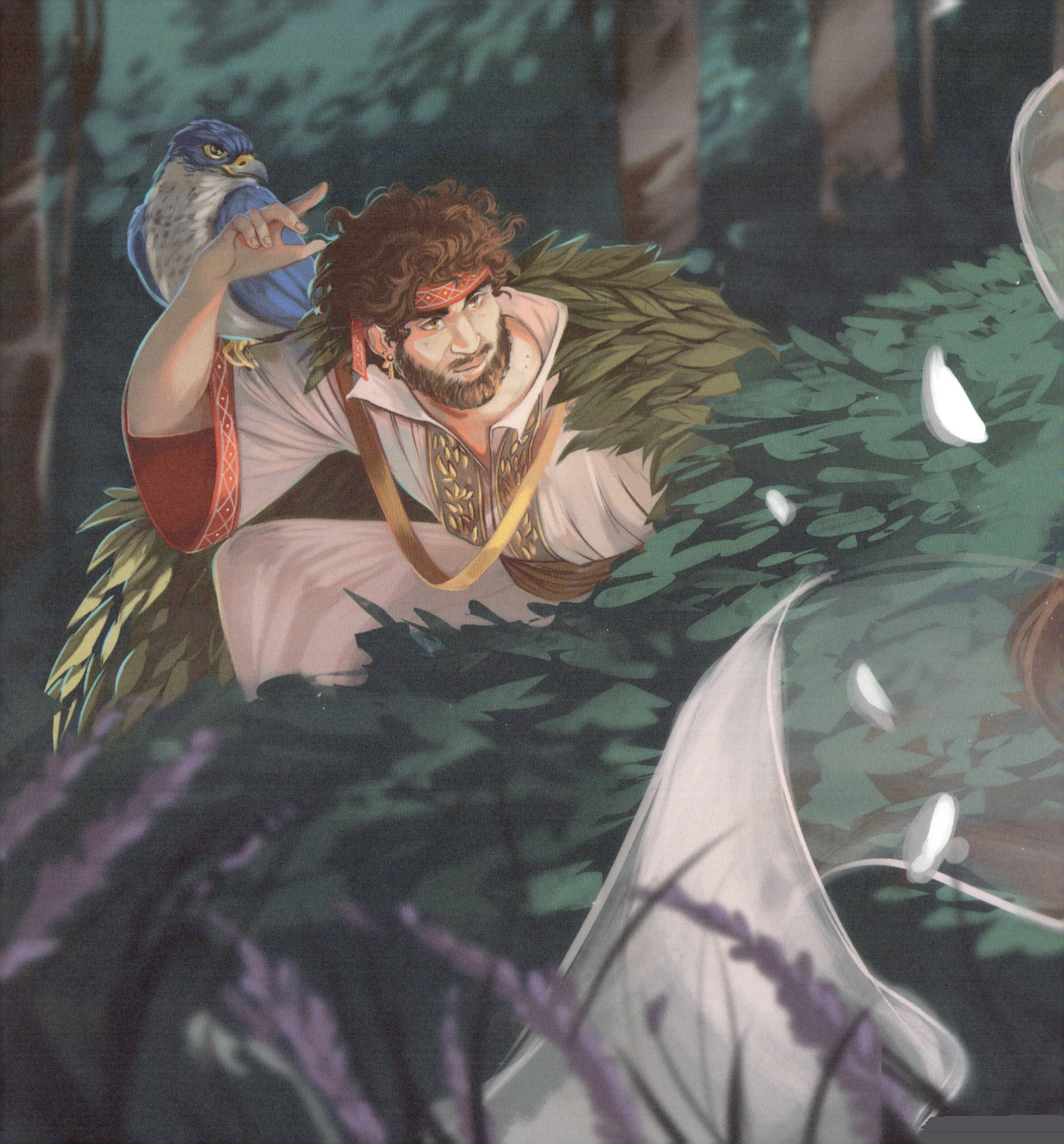

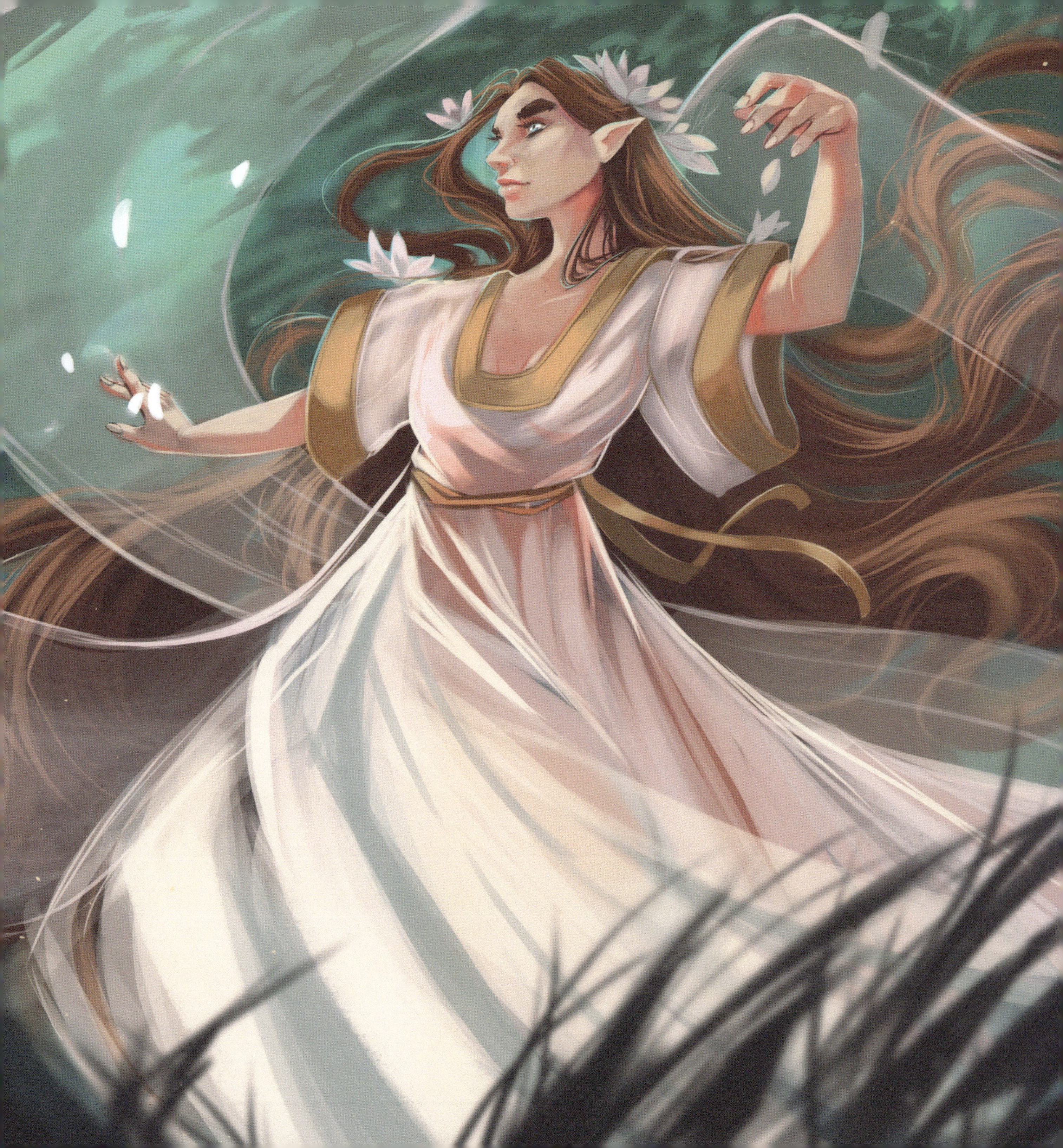

umphantly. Marko feared that his end was near, so he called Ravijojla, his sworn sister, who had promised to help him in case of danger. "Where are you, now that I am in need?" he called desperately, and a voice answered from the clouds. "Brother, to fight two against one would be dishonourable. Are you really unable to finish this foe on your own? Don't you have any weapons hidden in your robes?" she asked, reminding Marko that he did have a thin blade that he had not yet used. As Musa looked up at the sky, wondering about that mysterious voice, he did not see Marko quickly drawing his dagger from his clothes and plunging it into his enemy's chest. He then cut Musa's robes open and found that he had three hearts in his chest. The first heart had been pierced during the fight, the second had been wounded by the dagger, and the third was surrounded by a snake, which slept coiled around it. Suddenly the serpent aroused, and Musa's heart started beating again. His body writhed, startling Marko, while the serpent hissed menacingly in his direction, making it clear that if it had woken up during the fight, Musa would have been infinitely stronger. "Forgive me, Almighty God, for I am about to kill a warrior far more valiant than myself!" exclaimed Marko Kraljevich then, swinging his scimitar and cutting his enemy's head clean off before he could fully revive.

Marko owned a falcon to which he was very attached, but that was not the only bird of prey the hero was fond of. One day he was standing alone in the middle of the steppe, badly wounded after a fierce fight. He thrust his spear into the ground, leaning against it feverishly, but he did not have even the strength to stand up and so collapsed on the dry, dusty ground. The sun scorched his skin, and the heat dried his lips, so much so that he thought he would soon die. When he saw the shadow of a bird circling above him, he imagined that vultures had come to feed on his flesh. To his astonishment, instead, he noticed that it was an eagle that perched beside him and, bringing its beak close to his mouth, gushed out fresh spring water. Marko drank greedily, and then the bird of prey landed on the warrior's spear, spreading its wings and shielding him from the scorching light. Thus refreshed, Marko was able to fall asleep and regain his strength. While he was resting, a *vila* noticed the strange scene and approached the eagle, asking it what it was doing. "I'm helping my friend Marko Kraljevich, for when my wings were encrusted with blood and I couldn't fly, he removed me from the battlefield, where I would have been killed, and placed me safely in a tree. After some time, a refreshing rain washed away the dried blood from my feathers, allowing me to fly again. Marko also saved my babies, carrying them out of a burning castle and putting them on a tree, where I finally found them. This is the least I can do for such a hero!" The *vila* agreed and let the bird of prey take care of Marko. Sometime later, the knight was able to get up and thanked the kind bird, which then flew away, glad to have returned Marko's favours.

The sun was setting, and the hero noticed a beautiful maiden dancing with her companions in a clearing, their robes and feathered wings abandoned on the grass. He hid in the bushes, admiring this unusual scene, sure that he was watching nothing less than the dance of the vile. Then he sent his falcon swooping down to steal the wings of the most beautiful among them. At the sight of the bird of prey, all the nymphs flew away, but the one who had been left without wings remained behind, looking around in shock. When she saw Marko and the falcon he carried on his arm, she realised what must have happened. Angry and determined to retrieve her wings, she started chasing after the prince, but he was quick and did not let her catch him, at least not before he had shown her his extraordinary qualities. When the *vila* finally caught up with him, she was impressed by the hero's strength and cunning. Instead of asking for her wings back, she agreed to become his wife, on the condition that he would not reveal her true nature but always describe her as the simple daughter of a shepherd. The *vila*, named Nadanojla, lived with Marko for some time, and everybody was astounded by her fair appearance, persuaded that she was a nymph rather than an ordinary woman. However, the prince kept his word and continued to deny it, until Nadanojla gave him a son. At that point, full of joy and emotion, Marko could not contain himself and exclaimed that a *vila* had given birth to his heir, but in doing so, he broke his promise. Nadanojla regained her wings and flew away, but the poem tells how, later on, the hero sought her forgiveness and they finally got back together.

Marko Kraljevich had a long and adventurous life, but one day, while climbing a mountain on the back of his spotted horse, he felt it shake. Its legs refused to continue along the path, and copious tears were flowing from the creature's black eyes. "Šarac, my friend, what's wrong? We've been through so much together, and I have never seen you in these conditions" the knight said, worried. At that point, Ravijolja appeared at his side, stroking the steed's neck. "Oh brother, you really don't know why Šarac is in this state? He aches for you, for he knows that your time is near. For your fate has no violent death in store, no warrior will boast of having killed you, but your spirit will be extinguished on this very mountain. Do you disbelieve me? Well then, proceed along this path and stop at the spring between two tall pines. There you will discover the hour of your death". Marko did not want to believe her, and he spurred his horse, which with difficulty resumed the path, until they reached the trees that the *vila* had mentioned. Marko dismounted and approached the calm waters, trying to look at his reflection, but he could not see it. "So it is true, – he murmured sadly – I must die today". He caressed the muzzle of the good Šarac with affection. "You and I have always been inseparable, and I dare not think what will happen to you if I die here. You'll find another master that will mistreat you, or maybe you'll end up in the hands of an enemy of mine, who will make you feel his hatred for me. No, I can't bear that!" With these words, he drew his Damascus steel scimitar, he raised it in the glistening sunlight and brought it down on his dearest friend, his heart torn. Šarac waited patiently for the blow, as if it were his last will, and Marko buried him with all honours, weeping and ensuring his trusty steed that they would be united in death just as they had been in life. He then took his sword and spear, breaking them into four and seven parts, and then hurled the pieces in different directions, as far as he could, so that nobody would be able to hold his weapons. Finally, he took his war club and hurled it with all its strength into the sea, where it sank. "When my club returns to the shore, then it will be time for all the greatest heroes to return to earth, strong and valiant as they once were, and I shall walk among them" he said with prophetic ardour. Then he sat down under one of the pine trees, wrapped in his emerald cloak, and there, after a life of exalting deeds, he passed away, in peace, accompanied by birdsong and the silent tears of the vile. The peoples of the Balkans still await his return. Like King Arthur, who rests in Avalon waiting for the moment to come back, so will Marko return one day, riding his faithful Šarac and bringing an era of peace and joy. For now, he sleeps a long, peaceful sleep in the arms of the vile, the nymphs of the woods, waters, and winds.

THE HUNTER AND THE RUSALKA

The rusalka *is a Russian water nymph, quite similar to the* vila *of the Southern Slavs. Indeed, some believe that these maidens dwell in the waters in winter, while in summer they move to the forest clearings, becoming more like the vile. In some legends, they are described as the souls of maidens who either died before marriage or drowned, and who therefore seek revenge, luring the young men close to the shore and pulling them down into the deep. They cannot stay away from their element for too long, but if they take along their comb, which can produce a large amount of water, they can resist longer on the surface.*

Ivan was a humble seal fisher who lived in northern Russia, following his prey every winter as they migrated, in order to accumulate a large bounty to sell later in the spring. There, he would build himself a hut where he could spend those short but challenging months. Cold, loneliness, and melancholy often pervaded him, which is why he always played his balalaika after sunset. One evening, the oil lamp went out, but Ivan paid no attention to this and continued plucking the strings of his instrument, but suddenly he shuddered because he heard rustling noises around him, as if there was someone else in the hut. Frightened, he groped for the lamp and turned it on again, but he saw no one and thought it must have been a trick of his imagination. The same thing happened over and over again: when Ivan played in the dark, something around him moved, as if it were dancing to the sound of his music, and the more time passed, the more curious Ivan became as to who or what it was. Finally, one evening, he lit the lamp but hid it behind a thick curtain to obscure its light; then, he started playing, ready to remove the cloth as soon as he heard something strange. Suddenly the light flooded the small hut, and a beautiful maiden winced, caught right in the middle of a dance. Since she had now been discovered, she confided to Ivan that she was a *rusalka* and could only stay out of the water for a limited time and show herself to a single person. Ivan fell madly in love with her and asked her to stay in his hut, and so she did, at least during the few hours when she could stay on dry land.

The two spent the whole winter together, but when the warm season came, instead of his usual trepidation, Ivan felt a deep sadness. His people were waiting for him back home, and he had gathered many seal furs that he needed to sell. He bade farewell to the *rusalka*, promising to return the following winter, and he walked back home mournfully. The water nymph had told him how to find her: he had to climb a tree bending over the water's edge and wait for the midday sun, whose reflection would show him where to dive. Ivan could not wait until the following year and tried much earlier to follow her instructions, because he could not bear to stay away from his beloved. He left his business and said goodbye to his family, then went to the spot where the tree stood, and at noon he dived into the water and kept swimming downwards, until, among the thick seaweeds, he felt something tugging at him. It was not the water plants, but his *rusalka*! Ivan stayed with her for some time, but the depths were not the right place for him, and he soon felt homesick. He knew she would not let him leave, so he began to feel like her prisoner. In the end, he did the only thing that, according to what he had heard by the villagers, could protect someone from a *rusalka*: the sign of the cross. At that point, he was suddenly thrown out of the water and was able to return to his village; but later, even when he went to the tree again, following the correct instructions, he was never able to see his *rusalka* again.

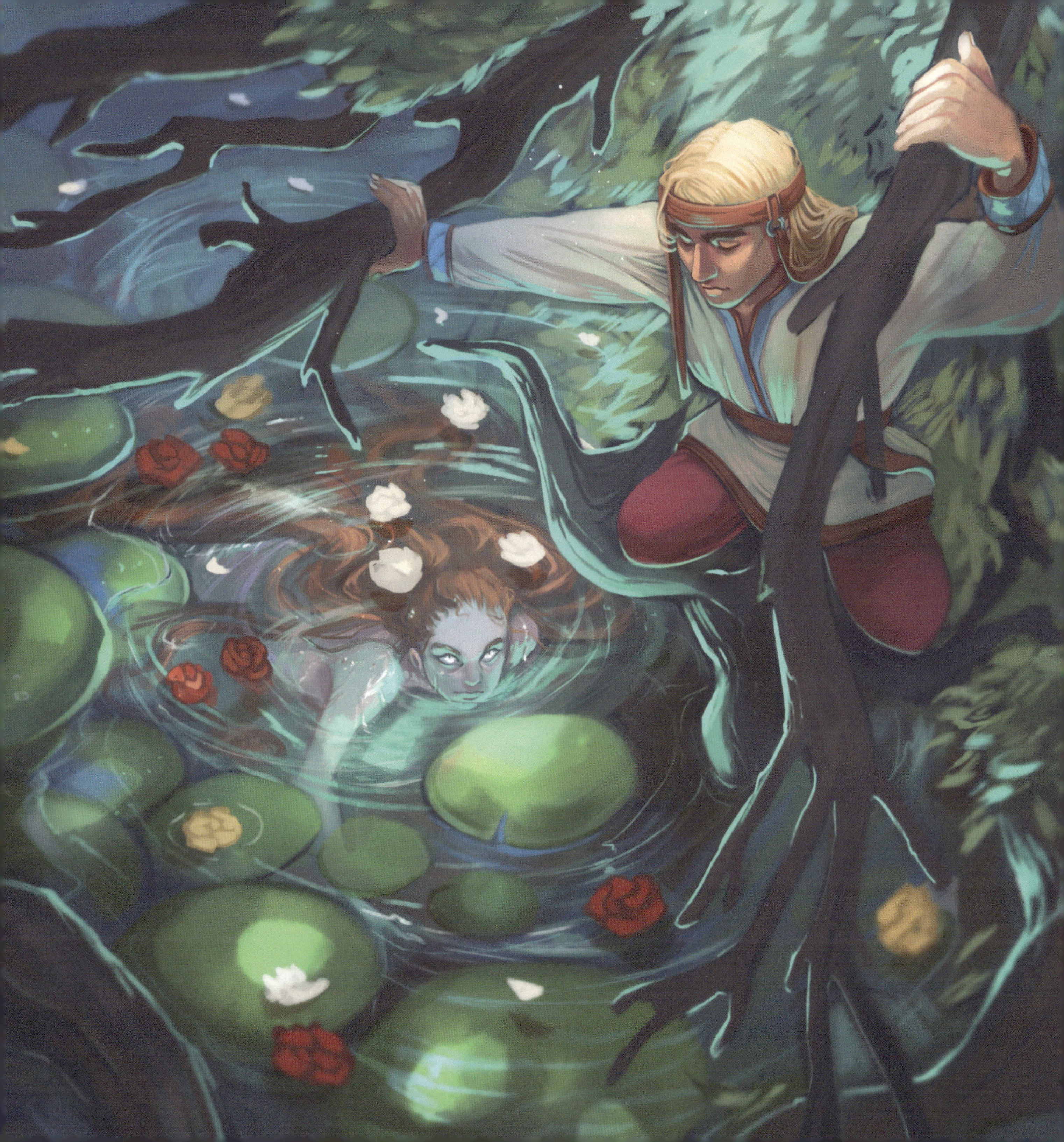

THE SWORD OF THE TWO LESHIYE

The leshi *(plural:* leshiye*) is a woodland creature whose name means "He Who Comes from the Forest". He is often represented with horns on his head, covered in foliage and bark, and accompanied by bears and wolves. Albeit occasionally gentle, he still has no pity for those who disrespect the forest. He can take the form of any animal he wishes, or even a human being, but he is not used to civilisation and tends to wear his clothes backwards and his shoes on the wrong foot.*

The sorcerer Nemal Chelovek had kidnapped the tsar's daughter, and it was rumoured that whoever brought the princess home safe and sound would receive her hand in marriage. Nonetheless, nobody had yet managed to find out where the girl was. One evening, while the simple soldier Ivan was keeping watch in the palace garden, he heard two crows talking to each other. The birds had witnessed the abduction and knew where the sorcerer had taken the girl. Ivan immediately ran to the tsar and asked permission to leave in search of his daughter. The tsar did not seem convinced to send a humble guard on a mission that had seen princes and knights fail, but he had nothing to lose and finally agreed. Ivan then took to the sea, following the directions he had overheard in the conversation between the two ravens, but he had to stop on an island to collect provisions and fresh water. While looking for a spring in the woods, he heard loud rustling and snapping noises, so he hid and saw that two *leshiye* were fighting.

They were tall and mighty, covered in foliage, their skin hard and wrinkly like bark, and on top of that, they seemed very angry. "The Samosek sword belongs to me! I inherited it thirty years ago!" bellowed one of them. "But you don't even know how to use it! Before I told you, you had no idea it could strike and move on its own, so you aren't worthy of it. That sword is mine!" replied the other. Ivan listened with interest, then decided to come out into the open, his hands well up in the air, making it clear that he came in peace. "Gentlemen, I couldn't help but overhear your arguing, and I can help you find a solution. I'll put you through a test to see which one of you is worthy of the sword. I will shoot an arrow into the woods, as far as I can, and the first one to bring it back can keep Samosek. What do you say?" he suggested, and the *leshiye* agreed. As he had said, Ivan nocked an arrow and stretched his bow, aiming upwards, beyond the foliage of the trees, then he let go of the string, and the arrow took off and disappeared from sight. The *leshiye* immediately ran after it, but Ivan did not wait for them to return; instead, he quickly grabbed the Samosek sword and returned to the ship, asking the crew to leave immediately, without provisions but with a formidable weapon.

After a couple of days at sea, they reached the island where the sorcerer had taken the tsar's daughter. Ivan, sword in hand, broke into the fortress, fearlessly confronting all those who tried to hinder him. The Samosek blade danced in the air, leaving its bearer's hand to make swift lunges and get rid of one enemy after another, and then meekly returned to him. In this way, Nemal Chelovek was also easily defeated, so Ivan retrieved the princess and returned to the tsar. However, he had to overcome the prejudices against the marriage between a noblewoman and a simple soldier. The princes who had failed to bring the girl back did not accept that a commoner would marry her, and so they assembled an army and attempted to attack him. Still, they were annihilated by the Samosek blade, just like the sorcerer's monsters. Seeing that he could not beat Ivan, one of the princes resorted to trickery, sending a letter to the princess and explaining how humiliating it was for a woman of her rank to be the wife of a palace guard. If she followed the instructions in that letter, she would soon become the wife of a prince. The tsar's daughter was convinced and waited as instructed until Ivan was asleep to take possession of the magic sword, replacing it with a copy. When he faced the rival army again, Ivan realised he had a common weapon in his hands, so he was defeated and left for dead on the battlefield, while the royal wedding was already being prepared at the palace.

The poor soldier woke up a few days later, hungry and exhausted. He reached out for the first bush he found and picked some strange yellow berries. As he ate one, he felt a sudden sharp pain in his head. Shocked, he touched it and found that he had grown large horns. He swallowed a second berry to better understand their power, and the horns disappeared at once, just as quickly as they had come. This oddity gave him an idea, so he returned to the palace, disguised as a beggar, and persuaded one of the princess's handmaids to put one of the berries in her food. As soon as the tsar's daughter swallowed the small fruit, she immediately clutched her head in pain, and shortly afterwards the whole court looked at her in horror or laughed at her, as she had two large horns starting from her forehead. The woman withdrew to her chambers, crying, while the king promised all kinds of riches to whoever could cure her sudden misfortune. It was the moment Ivan had been waiting for. Disguised as a ragged old man, he told the tsar that he was a healer and could help the princess, but only if he could meet her alone. The tsar agreed, willing to do anything to see her cured. When Ivan was admitted to his wife's chambers, he took off his disguise and scolded her for her infidelity. "Those horns suit you, my dear, and if it were up to me, I would let you keep them, but I happen to possess the cure. I will only give it to you in exchange for my sword!" he said, finding full cooperation from his wife. Once he had received Samosek, Ivan gave the woman a berry, and she returned to her original form. "Thank you, my sweet husband, – she whimpered - I promise I'll never look for other men. I thought you were not noble enough for me, but I was wrong! You proved to be the noblest of them all". Ivan listened to those fine words, but they did not mean anything to him. "You and your family are treacherous and cruel people, so I banish you from the kingdom. Since I have saved you, married you, and now also healed you, I deserve a great reward. I will stay and reign as tsar and try to help the poor people, instead of living in luxury and vanity as you have always done, so start packing your bags" he commanded. Ivan then became the new tsar, and the whole kingdom enjoyed years of peace and prosperity, as he was both an honest ruler and an unbeatable warrior, thanks to the help of the Samosek sword.

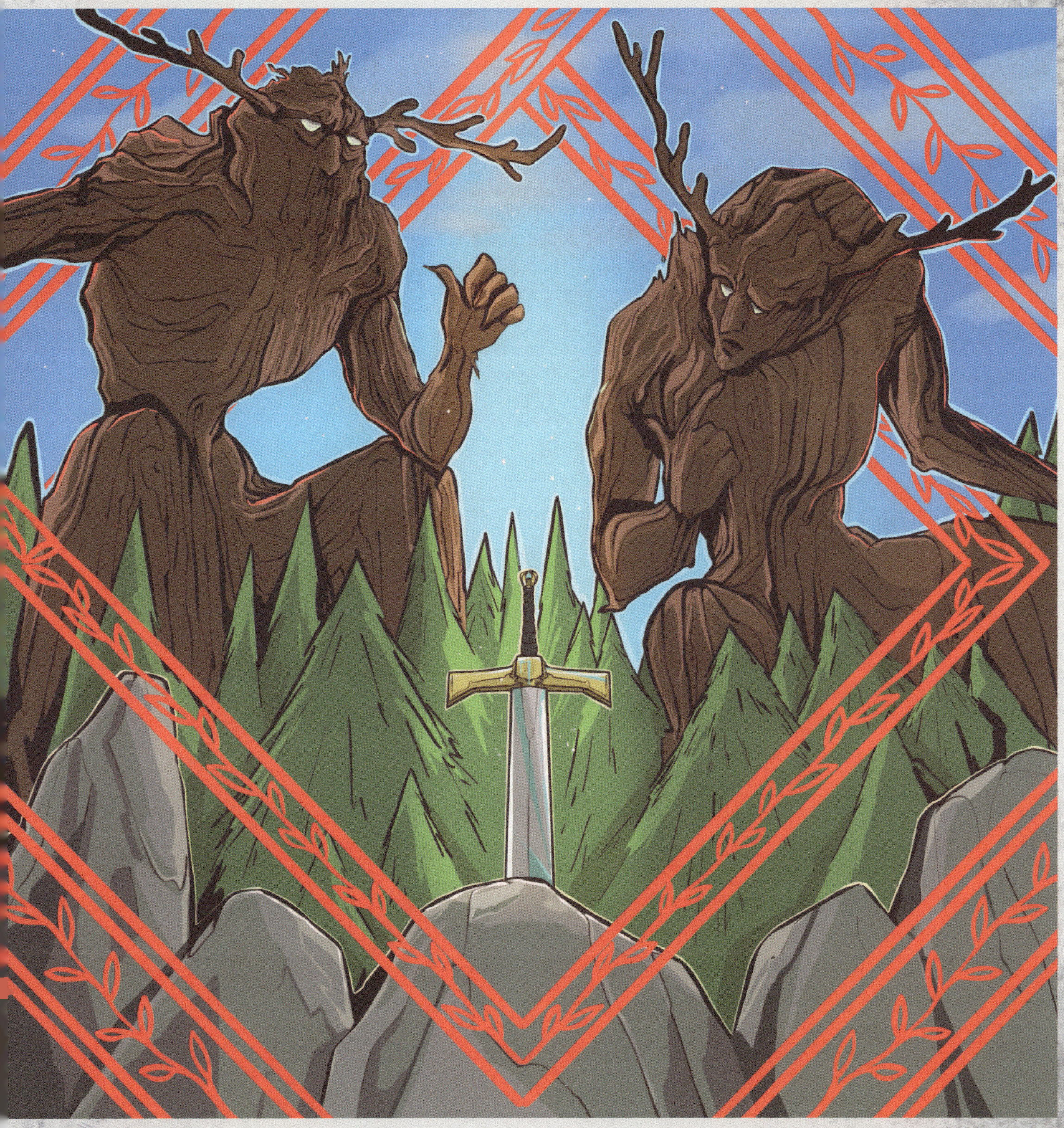

SVAROG AND THE DOMOVYE

The domovoy *(plural:* domovye*) is a domestic spirit that lives in the hearth or stove, the central point of the house where the family gathers. He protects the household members but may abandon or punish them if they misbehave. He is depicted as an old man with a long beard, a pointed nose and two cunning little eyes. Sometimes he wanders off at night in animal form (usually a cat or a dog), or he moves to the stables to tend sheep, cows, and horses, but he always returns to his abode afterwards. His judgment was highly valued: every time the family acquired a new animal, they carried it in procession around the house, so that the* domovoy *could recognise it and place it under his protection.*

They say that the *domovye* used to be actual deities and that they protected the lineage to which they were attached, fighting each other for more resources and prosperity to the detriment of the others. They were the spirits of the mythical progenitors, the ancestors of a given family, and they tried to protect and benefit their people in every way. Their role was so essential that they were as important as Rod himself in the eyes of their descendants, and so they began to put on airs. At the dawn of the world, when human beings were still few and lived in small, remote villages, the *domovye* revolted against Svarog. Still, the creator-god grabbed his mighty hammer and easily chased them away, banishing them from the divine realm and causing them all to fall to earth. Some ended up in gardens, others in stoves, animal pens or fields, and from that day on, they began to protect their lineage from close quarters, dwelling where they had fallen.

THE WOLF AND THE FIREBIRD

The Firebird (zhar-ptitsa) appears in many Russian fairy tales as a marvellous creature that the hero must find in order to complete his quest. It was represented as a falcon with a long peacock tail, whose feathers sparkled like a living flame and, even when detached from its body, were bright enough to lighten up a whole room.

Ivan Vyaslovich lived with his father and brothers in a rich palace surrounded by a magnificent garden. In the middle of this garden was a tree with golden apples, occasionally visited by the most extraordinary of creatures, the mythical Firebird. The tsar promised half the kingdom to the one of his three sons who would manage to capture the radiant bird. Two of them tried to guard the apple tree, but they fell asleep and did not even see the bird approaching, while Ivan managed not only to stay awake, but also to catch one of its long tail feathers. The bird flew away, but the boy could hand over the precious shiny feather to his father. But the tsar was not satisfied; in fact, the sight of that one feather only increased his desire to see the creature that possessed such a wonderful plumage. Thus, Ivan and his brothers set off in different directions looking for the mythical bird.

The hero found himself at a crossroads, whose signs promised certain death to anyone who proceeded to the left, and death to the horse of anyone who ventured to the right. The idea of losing his steed pained Ivan, but he had no other choice, so he took the path to the right, where a giant wolf soon attacked him. The horse fell to the ground, mortally wounded by the predator, while Ivan walked away, often looking back with regret. Suddenly, he noticed that the wolf was chasing him, and he feared he would soon end up like his horse, but the beast only wanted to apologise. "I hadn't eaten for days and was so hungry that I couldn't resist the sight of that succulent horse. Forgive me for taking away your travelling companion. If you wish, you can ride on my back, and I'll take

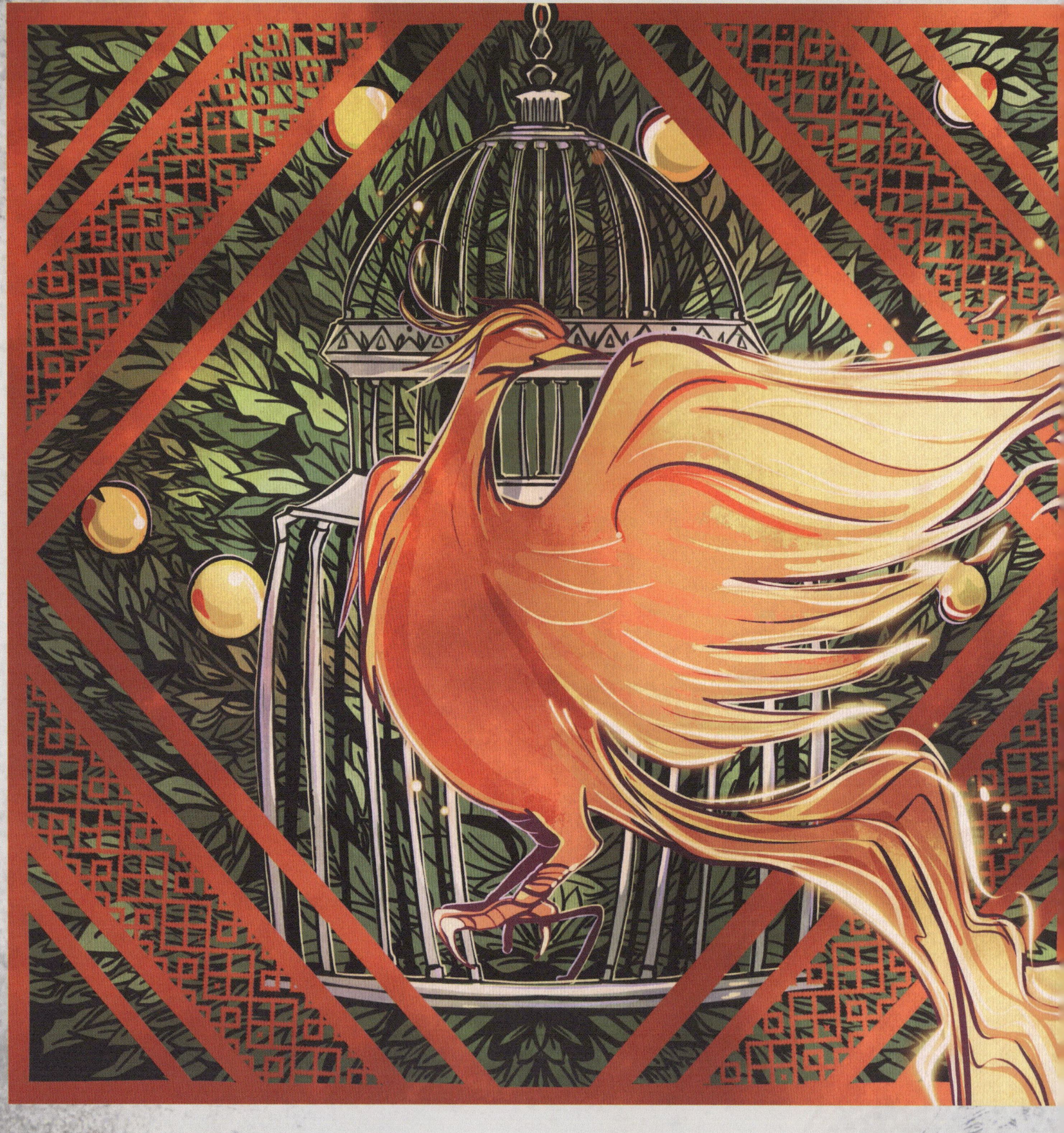

you wherever you want to go". Ivan was truly astonished by such a proposal, but he accepted, because the road was long, and he would never reach his destination on foot.

They came to Tsar Dalmat's huge palace, where the Firebird was kept in a golden cage encrusted with precious stones. Every night, the door was opened, allowing the creature to fly all over the world, but it always returned at dawn. The wolf let Ivan dismount and gave him some useful advice: "Sneak into the garden, where they keep the bird. Take it but don't remove anything else, not even the cage!" The young man nodded and slipped into the palace, where he found a beautiful garden that even surpassed his father's estate. Right in the middle was the precious cage, a treasure in its own right, with the mythical bird inside. Ivan remembered the wolf's advice, but the bird might have flown away without its cage; moreover, he thought, it was so beautiful that it would have been a shame to leave it behind. He grabbed everything and made to leave in a hurry, but at the entrance, he found Tsar Dalmat's guards, who seized him like a petty thief. The lord of that palace threatened to throw Ivan into the dungeon, but he was willing to spare him on one condition. "Since you are so good at sneaking into other people's palaces, bring me the Golden-coated Filly that lies in the stables of Tsar Afron". The boy had no choice but to accept.
Luckily, the wolf knew the way, and once again warned him: "Take only the filly and nothing else!" Ivan reached the stables where the most beautiful filly he had ever seen was resting. Hanging from a hook were bridles made of pure gold, and the boy thought that it would be difficult to ride the animal without them, and they were also very valuable. Once again, he disobeyed the wolf and was then captured by Tsar Afron, who would only release him if he brought him Princess Helena the Beautiful. The wolf was very displeased. "You can't even follow the simplest instructions! I should better retrieve the girl myself" he snorted. He leapt away and came back sometime later with the most delicate maiden of all Russia on his back. Ivan mounted behind her on the wolf's back, and as they travelled towards the palace of Tsar Afron, the two youngsters fell in love and were saddened by the thought that they would soon have to part. The princess's

tears moved the wolf, so he decided to help the naïve humans once more. He turned into an exact copy of Helena, then had Ivan take him to the tsar, who then agreed to let him ride off on the Golden-coated Filly.

The boy returned to the clearing where the real Helena was hidden and took her with him, but he often turned to look at the palace, regretting the loss of his dear wolf friend. Soon, though, he heard the sound of four agile paws running behind them. The wolf had returned! Thanks to his enormous powers, they managed to trick Tsar Dalmat as well, pretending to deliver the filly, when in fact it was the wolf, so that they could walk away with everything: princess, mare, and Firebird. Ivan did not know how to thank the wolf, but suddenly he noticed a horse's skull on the ground and realised that this was the spot where he had first met the grey-coated friend. At that point, the wolf sat down. "I can go no further. Here we have met, and here we have to part ways" he said solemnly. Ivan thanked him from the bottom of his heart, sinking his hands into his warm fur and hugging him tightly. Then, with a heavy heart, he took the golden reins of the filly that was carrying Helena and headed for his own kingdom.

His two brothers saw him arrive with a beautiful maiden, a cage containing a being of pure light, and a filly whose coat glittered like gold, and they turned green with envy. With a knowing glance, they agreed to attack Ivan, snatching the loot from him and then pretending to have retrieved it themselves. They threatened to kill Helena if she ever revealed the truth to the tsar, and left poor Ivan lifeless on the ground, a feast for crows and vultures. A long time passed in the steppe, and a flock of black birds had already gathered over the hero's body, but a howl chased them away, as the wolf ran and growled to disperse them. He grabbed the slower one with his fangs, offering to spare him on one condition. "I know that you feathered creatures know every place, since you can fly high in the sky and see everything. Bring me the Water of Life and Death to resurrect my friend Ivan, and then I will save your life. Don't try to deceive me, because I know where your nest is, and I've seen that it is full of young, featherless chicks…" Faced with that threat, the crow assured he would help him. He flew far away and returned a few hours later, carrying some drops of the miraculous water in his beak. As soon as the water sprinkled Ivan's body, he reopened his eyes, ready to return to the palace and take back Helena and the other treasures. The wolf that had done so much for him wished him luck, and his brothers turned pale as soon as their victim walked into the vast hall. Helena wept with joy and revealed everything that had happened to the tsar. The two evil brothers were locked in the dungeon, while Ivan and the maiden were finally able to marry and inherit the kingdom.

FINIST THE FALCON

Several Russian fairy tales tell of a splendid prince that was turned into a hawk, Finist the Falcon. One of these tales also features Baba Yaga, the witch who lives in the heart of the forest. She is sometimes said to fly inside her mortar. She has an evil nature, connected to winter, sterility and death, but also a benevolent one, just like all the ancient figures linked to the seasonal cycle and the harvest. Baba Yaga, indeed, seems to be the relic of ancient many-faced mother goddesses, who could be either helpful or vengeful.

In Russia, there lived a man with his three daughters. One day, as he was going to the market, he asked them what gifts they wanted. The two eldest girls approached him enthusiastically, asking for clothes and ornaments, while the third remained aloof, and when her father asked what she wanted, she humbly replied: "All I need is a little red flower". The sisters laughed at her, and even her father tried to change her mind, inviting her to ask for something more valuable, but she would not hear of it. When the man reached the market, he tried to find something to please all his daughters, but although he could buy fine clothes, necklaces, and fabrics, he could not find anyone selling flowers. Finally, on his way home, he met a man carrying one in his jacket: a small red flower just as his daughter had asked for. He approached him and offered to pay dearly for the flower, but the other shook his head. "This flower is not for sale, but I will give it as a gift to the girl who will marry my son". The man then revealed he was asking it for his youngest daughter, and that he was willing to give her in marriage in exchange for that little flower. "All right, – said the wayfarer – I'll send my son to meet her soon". And so the negotiation was concluded, and all three girls received the gift they desired.

The youngest was pleased with the red flower and put it on her windowsill, but something strange happened that evening. The maiden heard a flapping of wings, then a falcon glided into her room and, as soon as it touched the ground, turned into a beautiful young man. "My name is Finist, – he introduced himself, bowing – and I have come to meet my bride. I followed the red flower". The girl blushed, because Finist was indeed handsome, and she could not have found a better husband. She introduced herself in turn, and the two spent the evening together, realising they had strong feelings for each other. "I must go now, – the boy finally said – but I'll come back to see you every night, if you wish, as long as the flower is on your window. I leave you this feather of mine as a token: all you have to do is shake it to get whatever you want". With these words, he kissed her and disappeared in a flurry of feathers. As promised, Finist returned in secret every night, and the feather really did fulfil every wish. Thanks to it, the girl could travel in a splendid chariot driven by white steeds and walk around the city square dressed as a real princess, with jewels and precious silks, without ever being recognised.

Her sisters gossiped, wondering who this mysterious girl was, until one day they noticed a diamond pin that the little sister had forgotten to take out of her hair. This made them so suspicious that they started eavesdropping at the door of her room and discovered that, every night, the voice of a young man could be heard. "Maybe he's the one giving her all those riches. It's not fair!" exclaimed one of them. "You're right; we have to teach him a lesson!" replied the other. The next day, they waited for their sister to leave the house, then set a trap on the window, placing well-hidden blades. That evening, when Finist the Falcon flew towards his beloved, the blades wounded his wings, and the maiden found herself holding a young man covered in blood in her arms. Before realising what had happened, Finist flew away, resuming his bird form and flying painfully back to his home. The youngest sister wept bitterly, and her tears grew even more bitter the following nights, when no one came to her window. In the end, she decided to set out and search for Finist, to explain to him that she was innocent and willing to help him heal. She was only a young girl, and the world was full of danger, but she was not afraid; the only thing that mattered to her was finding Finist.

After wandering for a long time, she realised that she had lost her way in the forest, and would surely have died of hunger and cold, had she not followed the smoke she saw rising above the foliage from some fireplace. She found herself in front of a truly bizarre little house: it stood on huge chicken legs and could move at will. "Please, little house, turn your door towards me. I need a warm, dry place to rest!" she begged, and the cabin seemed to hear her, since it turned around and lowered itself, showing her the entrance. The interior smelled of herbs and mosses, a spinning wheel stood in one corner, a fire crackled in the fireplace, and a crooked old woman was working with mortar and pestle. She had a long, hooked nose and sharp teeth like a predator, dishevelled hair that looked like a bunch of snakes, and a sharp, disturbing gaze. Only then did the girl notice the bones that the old woman had arranged around her house like a fence, and she started to feel scared. The old hag, who was none other than Baba Yaga, sniffed the air with a guarded expression. "It's been years since the smell of Russia reached this place, but now I can smell it clearly! Who are you, and what do you want? Are you running away from a tiresome job, or are you looking for one?" she inquired, approaching the young girl hastily. The girl resolutely explained that she had set out to find Finist the Falcon, at which point Baba Yaga showed her own benevolent side, the one inherited from the ancient goddesses of fertility and the earth. "Sit down, child, and eat something. You will rest by the fire tonight, but in the morning, you'll set out to the sea. I have heard that a marriage is about to take place between Finist and the tsar's daughter who lives in those lands, but don't look so downcast! Take these precious stones and offer them to the princess for the chance to look at Finist once more. Then you can

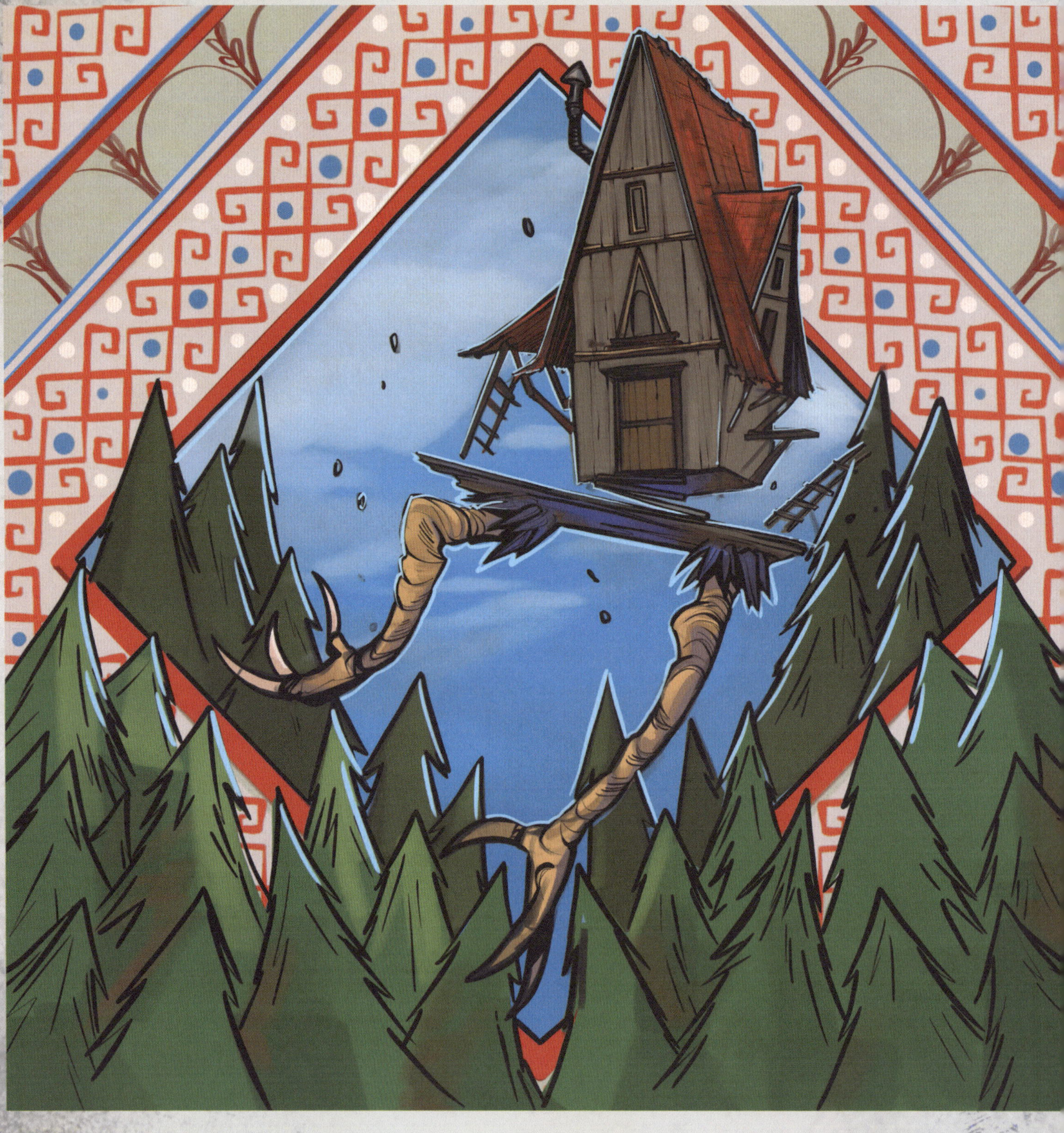

explain everything to him," said the wise lady.

The girl took some rest and then resumed her journey until she reached the lands near the sea, where she introduced herself as a merchant of precious stones. The princess was delighted to look at her splendid goods, and even more pleased to learn that she would get them as gifts if she showed her betrothed to that merchant while he slept. The princess told the maidservants to let her pass, but first she took precautions, putting in Finist's hair a magic clip that would keep him sound asleep. When the girl was allowed to see her beloved again, she shook him to wake him and tell him what had happened, but Finist was just lying there like dead. She started crying then, resting her forehead on his chest and stroking his hair, fearing that she had lost him forever. Finally, thanks to that very act, she found the clasp with her fingers and removed it. This time she shed many tears of joy as Finist opened his eyes again. At first, he did not seem pleased to see her, but when she explained everything to him, the young man stood up and summoned his second betrothed. "I find myself in a difficult situation, for I have promised to marry both of you, but now I must choose only one. Who shall I keep with me? The one who sold me for gold and jewels, or the one who bought me, giving up all her fortune? I have no doubt, and now that I know it was a trap set by your envious sisters, I can finally marry you!" After her long wanderings, the maiden had found her beloved, and as they had planned from the start, before the sisters ruined everything, the two celebrated a grandiose wedding.

MARYA MOREVNA AND KOSHEI THE DEATHLESS

Koschei The Deathless is a typical antagonist of the byliny. *His character may be based on Khan Končak, a historical figure from the 12th century, leader of the Polovtsians and present in* the Tale of Igor's Campaign, *where he captures and pursues the protagonist. He lived an exceptionally long life, which may have inspired the legend of his immortality. The egg that was said to contain his life re-*

sembles the oval-shaped protective amulets used by the Turkic peoples. In Russian, "Koščej" means captive and skinny, bony, skeleton-like, but also greedy, and this term is used to describe Khan Končak in The Tale of Igor's Campaign. *This may explain the origin of the name of the chthonic Deathless Koschei.*

Ivan Tsarevich was the son of the tsar, as his name indicates, and he had three sisters. Before he died, his father made him promise to find a good husband for the three girls as soon as possible, and the boy replied that he would not hesitate to marry them off to the first satisfactory suitor. One day, while they were out for a walk, a storm cloud appeared on the horizon, and suddenly a hawk swooped down and turned into a prince. After bowing and introducing himself, he asked for the hand of one of the princesses, and Ivan agreed, seeing that his sister was attracted to the young man. Sometime later, the same thing happened with an eagle that came ashore and became another suitor, this time for the second sister. Finally, the third girl also got married; in this case, her suitor was a prince who had presented himself as a raven. Ivan then remained alone, and after a few months, he decided to set out to see his dear sisters again. He came across a large battlefield, where it was clear that a boundless army had defeated an equally powerful enemy. In the distance, he could still see the victors' camp and hear celebration noises. Thus, he went closer and found that this army followed the warrior princess Marya Morevna. He insisted on meeting her in person, and she welcomed him for a few days as an honoured guest, even allowing him to sleep in her luxurious tent, but she advised him never to open the chest she kept in the corner.

Naturally, as Ivan was overcome by curiosity, this was the first thing he did as soon as his lover left. In the chest, he found a man bound by twelve chains, who begged for a single sip of water. Ivan thought he would do no harm by giving the prisoner a drink, but as soon as the first drops touched his lips, he gained extraordinary strength and shattered the locks that held him prisoner. He uprooted the tent and ran away, sweeping up Marya Morevna along the way and carrying her with him like a whirlwind. Regretting his action, Ivan resumed his journey to find his sisters, and finally saw the hawk, the eagle, and the raven perched on an oak tree. He told them what had happened and discovered that the prisoner was none other than Koschei the Deathless, whom Marya Morevna had managed to capture with much effort and after a great fight. Now the maiden was his prisoner, and it was impossible to ascertain where Koschei had taken her. However, Ivan was determined to find her, and the three birds asked him for a token each, so that they might remember him and know if he was well. To the raven he gave a silver spoon, to the eagle a fork, and to the crow a golden ring, thanking them and resuming his journey after briefly hugging his sisters again.

He wandered for a long time before discovering where Koschei was keeping Marya Morevna and, while his rival was absent, freed her and took her away with him. When the Deathless returned to his hideout and did not find his prisoner, he sought advice from his wise horse, who taught him how to prepare a loaf of bread that would make anyone who ate it unbeatable. With that, not only did he catch up with the fugitives in no time, but he also defeated his rival in combat. "I could kill you, – he said to Ivan – but I am grateful to you for freeing me from my chains, so I will grant you my forgiveness three times". Having said this, he took Marya Morevna with him and returned to his lair. Ivan, however, did not give up and waited until his wounds had healed, then returned to take back his beloved lady, sneaking into Koschei's abode when he was hunting. The Deathless One's steed advised him again, explaining how to brew a miraculous ale that made him immensely strong. Thus, he caught up with the two fugitives in a few quick leaps, beating Ivan in a duel but sparing his life, because he owed him two more favours. After the third time, however, he was not so merciful: he tore the stubborn hero to pieces and, for good measure, he put him in a chest which he threw into the sea, confident that he would never see him again.

Meanwhile, the silver spoon and fork turned dark, and even the ring seemed to rust, showing the three birds that their brother-in-law had been seriously hurt.

They took flight to look for him, and the eagle dived into the sea, retrieving the box, while the hawk fetched the Water of Life and the raven the Water of Death, with which they sprinkled the remains of poor Ivan, bringing him back to life. "Luckily, you're well now, – they said, settling down beside him – but you'd better leave Marya Morevna alone. Koschei is too strong, and the advice of his horse makes him even more fearsome. You'd better come home with us". Ivan, however, did not agree. "I won't give up. I bet that if I also had a steed like Koschei's, I could beat him in no time!" He set off again at once, and when he found his beloved, he did not take her with him, but told her to investigate the origin of the mysterious steed. When the two met again, in great secrecy, Marya Morevna gave Ivan a cloth. "It took me a long time to gain Koschei's trust, but he finally told me where he found that horse. Apparently, beyond a river of fire, there is a hut where the witch Baba Yaga lives. Koschei knows her; he worked in her service long ago, looking after her daughters, who are actually beautiful mares. In the end, to reward him, the witch gave him a foal, which is now his trusty steed. Who knows, perhaps it was Baba Yaga herself who made him immortal…" Ivan interrupted her, his head full of doubts. "You spoke of a river of fire, but how did Koschei cross it?" Marya Morevna pointed to the cloth and said: "Shake it three times to the right, and a solid bridge will appear. Koschei always wears it to cover his head, but I managed to steal it from him, and I hope it will help you!" The two said their goodbyes, hoping to be reunited soon, then Ivan set off towards the distant lands where the fiery river was said to flow.

He was tired and hungry, and when he saw a small bird perched on a twig, he decided to kill it and cook it, but the little animal begged for mercy, promising to help him whenever he needed it. Attached to the bark of a tree was a beehive overflowing with good honey, so the hero approached it, but the bees promised to come to his rescue if he left them alone. So he kept going, his stomach grumbling, until he found a lost lion cub. Such was his hunger that he was going to roast that cub, but a larger lion appeared along the path, demanding the cub back and offering his services in return, should Ivan need them. Still hungry, but with the awareness that he could count on all those animals, he reached the banks of the river of fire, which exhaled hot gasses and could burn anything to a crisp at once. Thanks to Koschei's cloth, Ivan magically summoned a bridge to cross it and reached a hut surrounded by a fence made of bones, just as Marya Morevna had told him. There were twelve spikes around it, with human heads on eleven of them, but what disturbed Ivan the most was the fact that the last one was empty. He entered, greeting Baba Yaga politely and saying that he had come there to work in the stables and look after the horses. The hag greeted him with a grin. "All right, you will start tomorrow, but if you don't do your job well, I will use your head to decorate my fence!"

Ivan then ate a frugal supper and went to sleep, but at dawn, he went out to the pastures with the witch's magnificent mares. She had strongly recommended not to lose any of them, so Ivan set out to count them, but the mares galloped away in all directions, and he could not reach them all. He tried to chase them for hours, but they were too fast, and in the end, he fell to the ground, exhausted and weeping. He fell asleep with his face wet with tears, but the chirp of a bird woke him up. "What are you doing there on the ground, Ivan? Go to the stable: the sun is setting, and the mares have already gone home." The hero, amazed and quite relieved, leapt to his feet and set off, while Baba Yaga scolded her daughters harshly. "Why did you come back here? You know the routine! You had to run in every direction, so that I could kill him," she croaked. "How could we stay out there, with all those birds flying around us, trying to peck our eyes out and pushing us in this direction? At least we're safe in here," they grumbled. "Tomorrow, you must go into the deep forest, among the plants and the weeds, where those pesky birds can't follow you," suggested Baba Yaga, and then she prepared to welcome Ivan, pretending to be satisfied with his excellent work. The following day, the same thing happened again, as Ivan could not even reach the pastures before the mares disappeared. At nightfall, however, he found them all back in their stables, still frightened and trembling because of the ferocious beasts that had threatened them in the woods, led by a proud lion. That night, while Ivan slept, Baba Yaga gave his daughters another talk: "If all these animals torment you, run to the sea! You are supernatural creatures. Do

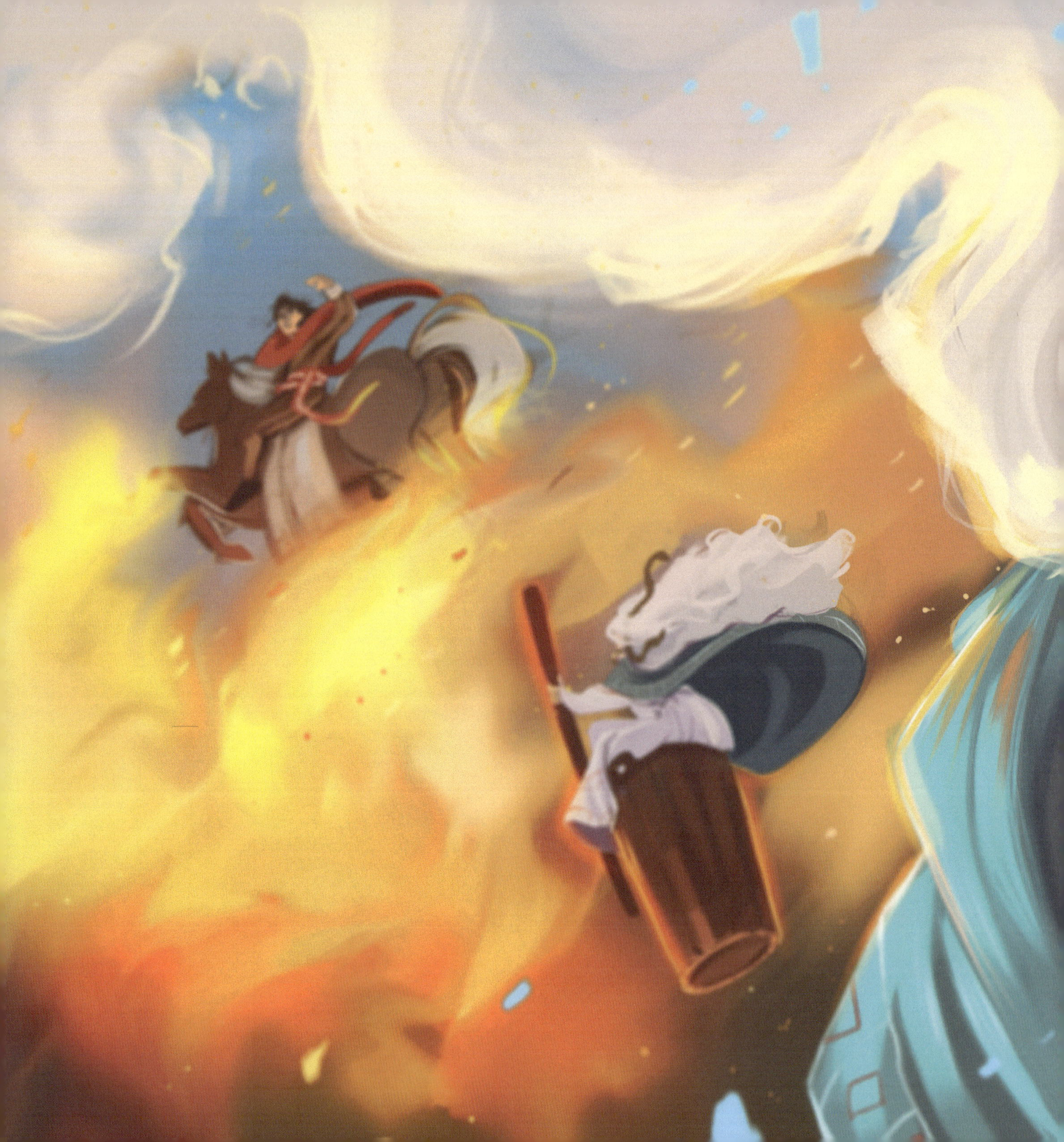

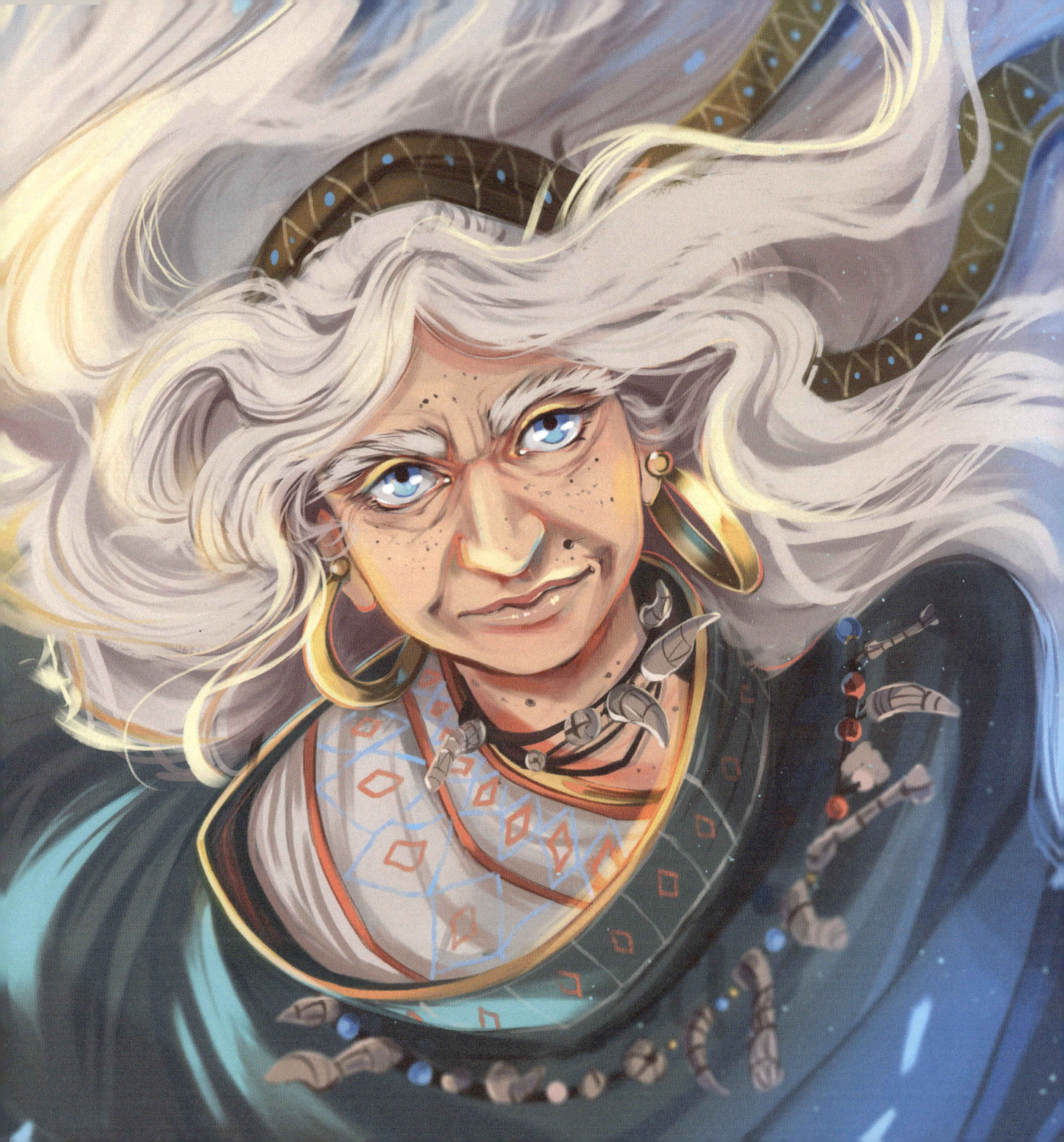

you know how to run on water, or have you forgotten?" The mares promised they would do everything they could to get rid of Ivan, and so, at dawn, they fled to the coast. This time Ivan feared that he had lost them forever, so he wept, looking at the distant waves, but he changed his mind when he heard a loud buzzing noise. A huge swarm of bees was chasing the mares, directing them precisely towards their stables. One of the bees landed on Ivan's shoulder and advised him: "Baba Yaga is trying to kill you, so you'd better leave". The hero replied that he had to finish the job to get a foal in return, just like Koschei had done. The bee then revealed to him that there was a young steed in the stables, and that Ivan should just take it and run away before the witch could notice the theft. The boy sneaked into the stables, saddled the horse, and then urged it to gallop as fast as possible towards the flaming river with its hot gasses. In the meantime, Baba Yaga had started looking for him, flying in her mortar and using the pestle as an oar to propel herself, clearing her tracks using a broom. When Ivan saw her approach, he shook Koschei's cloth three times to the right to create a bridge, but when he had reached the other shore, he shook it to the left, and the bridge disintegrated at once, so that the witch could not chase him any farther.

According to a variant of this story, Ivan managed to take Marya Morevna away on his wonderful steed. When Koschei chased them, against the wise advice of his own horse, he was killed by Ivan's new mount with a powerful hoof stroke. Another legend, however, dwells on the fact that Koschei could not die, and therefore the kidnapped princess had to discover his secret somehow. In this story, the maiden is said to have pretended to be worried about him and asked where his death was. Koschei, suspecting a trick, pointed to the first object he saw in his house, a broom. The next day, when he returned home after the hunt, he saw that she had decorated the broom with tufts and ribbons and left it on the table. "Have you gone mad? – he asked her, surprised – Why did you do that?" She explained that that broom, containing his soul, was a precious object and should be treated as such. Koschei snorted. "Do you really believe that my death could be in there? I lied to you. It's actually in that goat" he said, to test the princess and see if she would kill the animal while he was away. When he returned, he saw that she had washed the goat and combed its fur, covering it with ribbons, ornaments, and delicate fabrics. He could hardly keep from laughing. Apparently, the princess really wanted to safeguard the container of his soul, and he decided to reassure her: "You won't be able to adorn the place where my death lies, for it is kept inside a log that floats on the sea, in which a duck has nested. Inside her egg lies my soul, so I can't see how you could do anything about it". Ivan Tsarevich, who had rescued some animals, gained their friendship in this story as well, went to look for the log, which a mighty and helpful bear brought back to shore. The duck felt in danger and flew away at once, but a hawk swooped down and stopped her. Her egg fell into the sea, but a pike retrieved it and delivered it to Ivan. When the hero reached Koschei to get his beloved back, he kept juggling and fiddling with the egg, to his rival's dismay. In the end, he lost his grip, and the egg fell on the floor, cracking, and Koschei the Deathless collapsed to the ground, his skull split open just like the eggshell.

VAMPIRES AND WEREWOLVES

Vampires were known to the Slavic peoples as upyr. *This term designated a creature that, albeit dead, continued to torment the living and sucked their blood. To kill them once and for all, it was necessary to stab their chests with a hawthorn stake, since tradition had it that this plant could ward off negative influences. Alternatively, one could cut off their head. Vampires, in Slavic folklore, have much in common with werewolves, known as* vulkodlak, *human beings who are able to turn into wolves and who gather near the crossroads at night. In addition, both figures sometimes overlap with the* vedomci, *evil shape-shifting sorcerers who fight against the* kresniki *for the fate of the crops.*

The first person that the Slavic chronicles explicitly acknowledge as a vampire is Jure Grando, a villager who lived in Croatia in the 17th century. It was said that, although he had died of illness sixteen years earlier, he kept haunting the villagers. He used to visit his wife, who described him as a wheezing corpse with an eerie grin on his face, and he would knock on the doors of houses, causing the sudden death of the family members he had visited. At last, the parish priest gathered the villagers and tried to stop him. They surrounded him, holding up their crucifixes, and managed to drive a hawthorn stake through his chest. However, this method did not work because they could not drive it deep enough, so Jure managed to escape. Thus, they dug up his body and discovered that it was perfectly preserved and that it still displayed an eerie, hideous smile. When they cut off its head, blood gushed forth from the wound. The vampire started screaming and wriggling, but finally it lay down. From that moment, the villagers never saw or heard about him again.

Another case of vampirism occurred in Serbia, in the 18th century. The death of Petar Blagojevich was followed by nine more sudden deaths. The victims weakened and perished quickly, but on their deathbeds, they claimed that Petar had visited them at night and tried to strangle them. His wife said that she had found the vampire in the house one night, rummaging around and looking for something. As soon as he had seen her, he asked her to bring him his shoes. He also visited one of his sons to ask for food, and when the son refused, Petar assaulted him and fed on his blood, killing him. Terror gripped the entire village, so they unearthed the vampire's grave, finding that his body was still in perfect condition, and even his nails and hair had kept growing. His mouth was still smeared with blood, so the villagers attacked the corpse, staking it many times and thus resolving the problem. Sava Savanovich is another vampire said to have haunted some mill in Serbia, where he killed and sucked the blood of those who came to grind wheat.

In Slovenia we find the story of Žirovec, a wealthy man who continued to be seen by the villagers even after his burial. He also visited his wife at night and even had a child with her despite being a vampire. Even if he was a creature from the realm of the dead, Žirovec did not harm anyone. The villagers got used to seeing him, especially sitting on a stone near his house, wearing only one sock. However, the parish priest wanted to end this, so he opened the grave and drove a hawthorn stake through Žirovec's heart. The vampire then cried out in pain and died for good, but sometime later his wife gave birth to his son.

The character most associated with vampires is Vlad III, known as the Impaler, because of how he tortured and killed his prisoners, perhaps better known as Vlad Dracula. He was one of the most important rulers of Wallachia, a member of the Order of the Dragon, established to defend Christianity. His fame as a cruel and bloodthirsty man soon spread throughout the world, and during his lifetime, he fell and managed to regain power three times. He is the protagonist of many legends, and in Romania he is seen as a folk hero. Legend has it that even thieves were afraid of him and refused to steal a golden cup that Vlad had left unattended, so as not to face his wrath. One man asked for his help in recovering the ducats that had been stolen from him, and the fame of the ruthless Vlad ensured that he got them back immediately. Vlad gave him back one extra ducat, but the man humbly went back to hand over the coin that was not rightfully his. At that point, Vlad uttered a cruel laugh. "Very well, – he exclaimed – if you had not brought me back that coin, I would have impaled you along with the thief who stole all the others!" Even the monks feared him and went to pray at his grave to prevent his spirit from waking up and tormenting the living. It is also said that Sultan Mohammed II ordered to cut off the head from his corpse and hide his sword, for fear that he might come back to life and resume his raids. He was indeed a respected and feared man, yet in the numerous oldest sources we find no traces of a connection with vampirism. It was Bram Stoker, in his novel *Dracula*, who made this association, drawing inspiration from Vlad's turbulent personality and from Slavic folklore to create a character who has undoubtedly been able to fascinate and frighten readers for more than a century.
A medieval Greek tale, later translated into Russian Slavonic in the 12th century, describes the punishments inflicted on those who, instead of worshipping the one god, deified ordinary men such as Perun, who lived among the Greeks, Chors, a native of Cyprus, and Trojanu, a Roman emperor. Trojanu

also appears in *The Tale of Igor's Campaign*, and the Russians are described as his people. It may be the memory of Emperor Trajan, later turned into myth, but in Serbia there is a popular tradition about Trojan, a man of noble origins who lived in a castle, and who every night went in search of a young woman to be his lover. The sun's rays could have killed him, so as soon as he entered his lover's room, he would feed oats to his horse, being careful to leave as soon as it had all been eaten. He would also remain listening, ready to mount at the first cockcrow, to avoid the sunlight that would have burnt him to ashes. One day, the husband or the brother of the woman with whom Trojan lingered replaced the oats with sand and cut out the tongues of all the roosters in the village. Trojan did not notice how much time was passing, because the horse had not yet finished eating, nor had he heard the rooster crow. When he realised that morning was near, it was too late. He fled, hoping to reach his castle in time, but the sun's rays burned and almost destroyed him. He hid in a haystack, but the beasts came to eat the straw and knocked it over, exposing Trojan to the powerful light of day, which finally annihilated him. In this tale we find elements that will appear in the popular vampire tradition, such as the vampire looking for young women in the dead of night and his weakness to sunlight.

The term for a werewolf, *vulkodlak*, literally means Wolf Skin, and there seem to be connections with the Scandinavian *úlfhednar*, warriors who went into battle wearing wolf fur. We know that Kievan Rus', the first East Slavic state, was founded by the Varangians, Scandinavian peoples led by the three legendary brothers Rjurik, Sineus, and Truvor. They quickly merged with the Slavic population, which is why we find many elements of Scandinavian folklore in these lands. The *vulkodlak*, however, are much closer to the vampiric tradition, as it was believed that those who died in mortal sin would turn into bloodthirsty werewolves at night. At the first light of day, they would turn back into mere corpses, just like vampires did. To get rid of them, the body had to be decapitated and the head thrown into a river, where the weight of its sins would make it sink forever, but it was common to resort to the same remedies used against vampires. The *vulkodlak* are not only connected to the realm of the dead, however. Sometimes they are ordinary people, whose ability to turn into a wolf is revealed from birth by the presence of a particular mark, such as a spot on the skin, the placenta still wrapped around them, or thicker than normal hair, but it could also come about because of a curse. The time of transformation was usually marked by important seasonal events, such as solstices, equinoxes, or full moon nights. At the age of seven, they were ready to be welcomed into the group of werewolves, who would meet at night to hunt, damage crops, devour livestock, and pounce on the unfortunate who did not take shelter in their homes. In Serbia, there is a tradition according to which the *vulkodlak* would gather in winter, removing their wolf skins and hanging them on the frosty branches of trees. They would then choose one of those skins to burn, thus freeing one of them from the curse that turned him into a feral being.

In the chronicles, we find many characters said to have the power to turn into wolves. One of them is Bajan, son of the tsar of Bulgaria known as Simeon the Great. According to the historian Liutprand of Cremona, the young Bajan could become a wolf or some other animal. The Belarusian Vseslav was also described as having this ability, and Russian chronicles report that he was born through witchcraft, coming into the world with the placenta around his head. Powerful enchanters told his mother that this was a remarkable sign, and that to become strong and victorious, he should always carry a fragment of that placenta with him. According to the *Primary Chronicle*, this is why Vseslav was so bloodthirsty and warlike. When he began his massacres, a blood-red star would shine in the western sky, while the sun became pale and dull, more like the moon, and other terrible omens appeared in the lands of Rus'. The same prodigies are also described in the story of *Volkh Vseslavevich*, and we can imagine how the figure of the hero may have arisen thanks to the legendary aura surrounding this historically existent character.

As we have seen, Slavic tradition has many aspects due to the vastness of the regions inhabited by people of Slavic descent, each with its own peculiarities. It also contains references to Scandinavian, Iranian, and Finno-Ugric cultures, as well as various references to historical characters who later became legendary heroes. All this makes it a subject of considerable interest, a buried treasure that still has much to reveal, with its archaic gods, its dragon hunters, the vampires and werewolves that roam the night, the nymphs ready to guide the heroes to their destiny, and the other mysterious creatures that inhabit the lakes and forests.

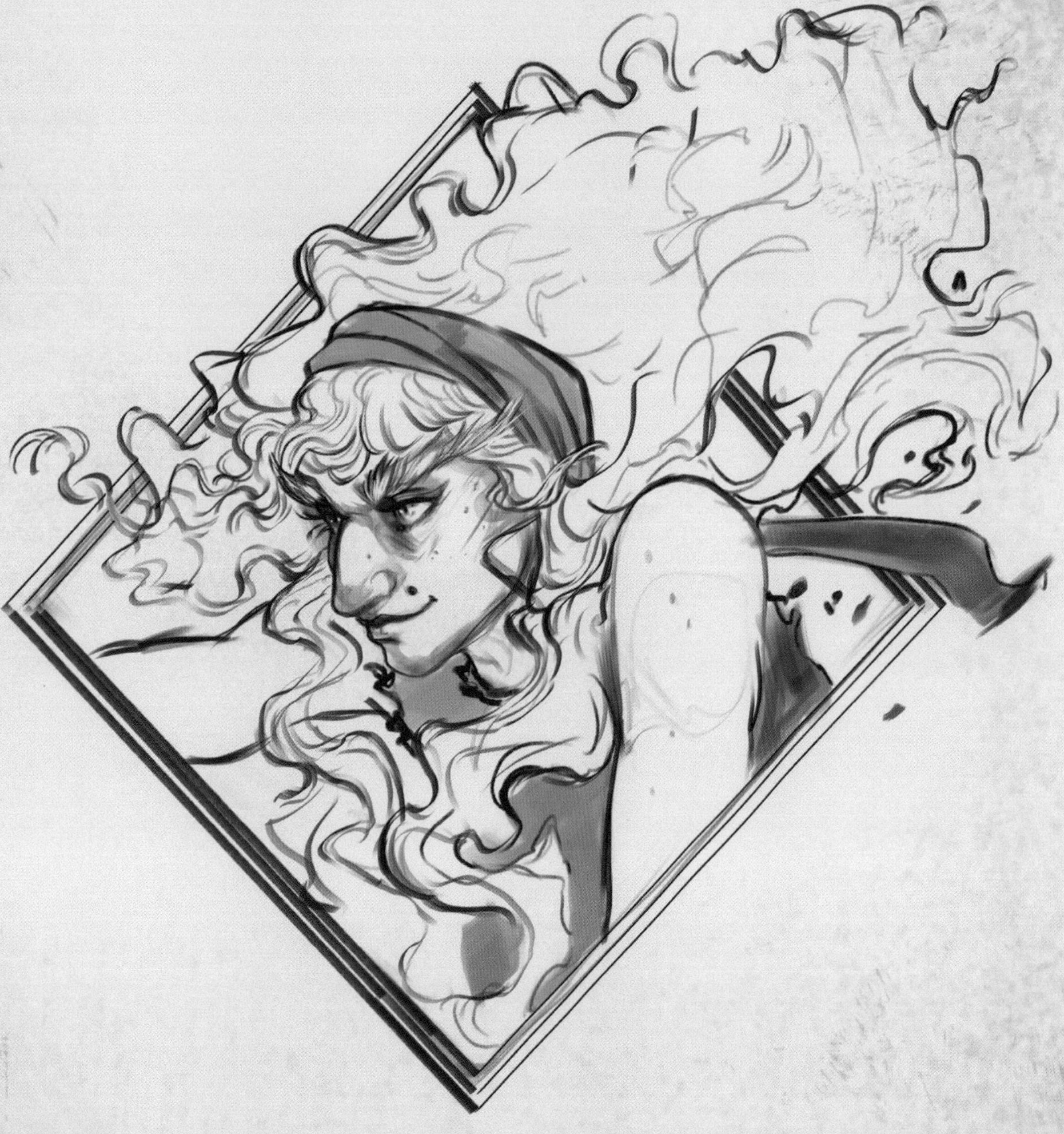

TEXTS TO EXPLORE FURTHER:

A. Bruckner, *Mitologia slava*

N. Chadwick, *The Beginning of Russian History: An Enquiry into Sources*

M. Dixon-Kennedy, *Encyclopedia of Russian and Slavic Myth and Legend*

M. Eliade, *Dizionario degli dei: Eurasia*

M. Gimbutas, *Ancient Slavic Religion*

J.V. Haney, *Russian Legends*

S. Hazzard Cross, *The Russian Primary Chronicle*

R. Jakobson, E. J. Simmons, *Russian Epic Studies*

A. G. Kossova, *All'Alba della Cultura Russa*

M. Kropej, Supernatural Beings from Slovenian Myth and Folktales
M. Kropej, *The Horse as a Cosmological Creature in the Slovene Mythopoetic Heritage*

M. Kropej, *The Tenth Child in Folk Tradition*

Léger, *La Mitologia Slava*

R. Mann, *The Igor Tale and Their Folkloric Background*

C. A. Manning, Marko, *The Kings Son*

B. Meriggi, *Le byline, canti popolari russi*

R. Picchio, *La Letteratura russa antica*

H. C. Puech, *Slavi, Balti, Germani*

P. Siminov, *Essential Russian Mythology*

S. Svetkovic, *Chernobog's Riddles*

E. Warner, *Dei, eroi e mostri della mitologia russa*

E. Warren, *Russian Myths*

YOU CAN ALSO FIND

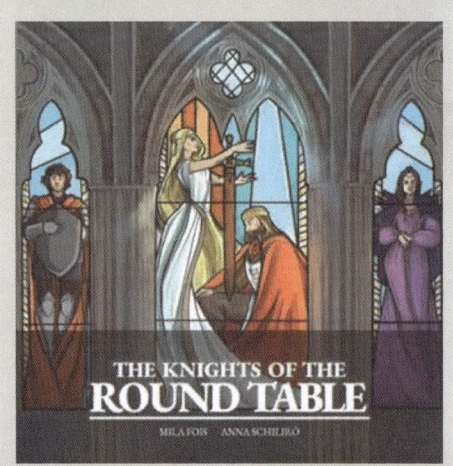

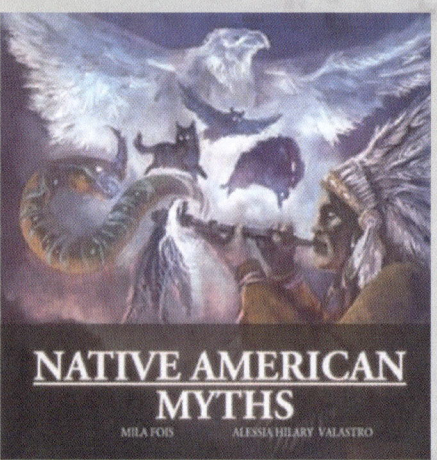

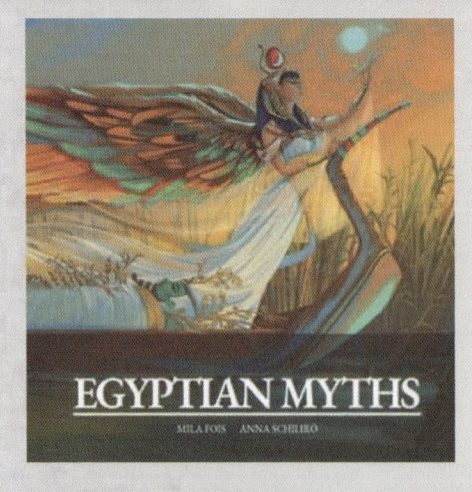

NORSE MYTHS
MILA FOIS — ALBERTO ORSO

CELTIC MYTHS
MILA FOIS — ALBERTO ORSO

TALES FROM KALEVALA
MILA FOIS — ALBERTO ORSO

JAPANESE MYTHS
MILA FOIS — ALBERTO ORSO

THE KNIGHTS OF THE ROUND TABLE
MILA FOIS — ANNA SCHILIRÒ

NATIVE AMERICAN MYTHS
MILA FOIS — ALESSIA HILARY VALASTRO

EGYPTIAN MYTHS
MILA FOIS — ANNA SCHILIRÒ

MYTHS AND CONSTELLATIONS
MILA FOIS — ASIA MARIANELLI

Thank you for reading this book!

SLAVIC MYTHS

Copyright © 2023 Mila Fois and Anna Schilirò

Head of publication Mila Fois

Printed in Great Britain
by Amazon